Ruth Rendell

———

"If there were a craft guild for writers, I'd apprentice
myself to Ruth Rendell."   —Sue Grafton

"The best mystery writer anywhere in the English-
speaking world."   —*The Boston Globe*

"Ruth Rendell is, unequivocally, the most brilliant mystery novelist of our time. Her stories are a lesson in a
human nature as capable of the most exotic love as it is
of the cruelest murder. She does not avert her gaze and
ma
an

"Re
sh
ta

"It
fo
pl
tio

"Ru

"Ruth Rendell is surely one of the greatest novelists presently at work in our language. She is a writer whose work should be read by anyone who enjoys either brilliant mystery—or distinguished literature."
—Scott Turow

"No one writes with more devastating accuracy about the world we live in and commit sin in today."
—John Mortimer

"Rendell's clear, shapely prose casts the mesmerizing spell of the confessional." —*The New Yorker*

"[Rendell] is a master at making the small English village into a metaphor for the world, understanding [its] workings . . . and how it relates to the violence surrounding us." —*The Dallas Morning News*

"No one can take you so totally into the recesses of the human mind as does Ruth Rendell."
—*The Christian Science Monitor*

"Rendell's prose, the psychological verity of her dialogue and her attention to telling details carry us through a whirlwind of adventure in a pretty unpleasant society that just may be microcosm of our own."
—*Pittsburgh Post-Gazette*

Ruth Rendell

The Fallen Curtain

The Fallen Curtain

The Fallen Curtain

Stories

Ruth Rendell

VINTAGE CRIME / BLACK LIZARD
Vintage Books
A Division of Random House, Inc. / New York

FIRST VINTAGE CRIME / BLACK LIZARD EDITION, JANUARY 2001

Copyright © 1976 by Ruth Rendell

All rights reserved under International and Pan-American
Copyright Conventions. Published in the United States
by Vintage Books, a division of Random House, Inc., New York.
Originally published in hardcover in the United States
by Doubleday, a division of Random House, Inc.,
New York, in 1976.

Vintage is a registered trademark and
Vintage Crime / Black Lizard and colophon
are trademarks of Random House, Inc.

Owing to limitations of space,
permission to reprint previously published material
can be found on page 187.

The Library of Congress has cataloged the Doubleday edition as follows:
Rendell, Ruth, 1930–
The fallen curtain : eleven mystery stories
by an Edgar-award winning writer / Ruth Rendell. —1st ed.
p. cm.
I. Title
PZ4.R4132 Fan 1976
823'.914 75-040739
CIP

Vintage ISBN: 0-375-70492-2

www.vintagebooks.com

Printed in the United States of America
10 9 8 7 6 5 4 3 2 1

Contents

The Fallen Curtain

The incident happened in the spring after his sixth birthday. His mother always referred to it as "that dreadful evening," and always is no exaggeration. She talked about it a lot, especially when he did well at anything, which was often, as he was good at school and at passing exams.

Showing her friends his swimming certificate or the prize he won for being top at geography: "When I think we might have lost Richard that dreadful evening! You have to believe there's Someone watching over us, don't you?" Clasping him in her arms: "He might have been killed—or worse." (A remarkable statement, this one.) "It doesn't bear thinking about."

Apparently it bore talking about. "If I'd told him once, I'd told him fifty times never to talk to strangers or get into cars. But boys will be boys, and he forgot all that when the time came. He was given sweets, of course, and *lured* into this car." Whispers at this point, meaning glances in his direction. "Threats and suggestions—persuaded into goodness knows what—I'll never know how we got him back alive."

What Richard couldn't understand was how his mother knew so much about it. She hadn't been there. Only he and the Man had been there, and he couldn't remember a thing about it. A curtain had fallen over that bit of his memory that held the details of that dreadful evening. He remembered only what had come immediately before it and immediately after.

They were living then in the South London suburb of Upfield, in a little terraced house in Petunia Street, he and his mother and his father. His mother had been over forty when he was born and he had no brothers or sisters. ("That's why we love you so much, Richard.") He wasn't allowed to play in the street with the other kids. ("You want to keep yourself to yourself, dear.") Round the corner in Lupin Street lived his gran, his father's mother. Gran never came to their house, though he thought his father would have liked it if she had.

"I wish you'd have my mother to tea on Sunday," he once heard his father say.

"If that woman sets foot in this house, Stan, I go out of it."

So gran never came to tea.

"I hope I know what's right, Stan, and I know better than to keep the boy away from his grandmother. You can have him round there once a week with you, so long as I don't have to come in contact with her."

That made three houses Richard was allowed into—his own, his gran's, and the house next door in Petunia Street where the Wilsons lived with their Brenda and their John. Sometimes he played in their garden with John, though it wasn't much fun, as Brenda, who was much older, nearly sixteen, was always bullying them and stopping them getting dirty. He and John were in the same class at school, but his mother wouldn't let him go to school alone with John, although it was only three streets away. She was very careful and nervous about him, was his mother, waiting outside the gates before school ended to walk him home with his hand tightly clasped in hers.

But once a week he didn't go straight home. He looked forward to Wednesdays because Wednesday evening was the one he spent at gran's, and because the time between his mother's leaving him and his arrival at gran's house was the only time he was ever free and by himself.

This was the way it was. His mother would meet him from school and they'd walk down Plumtree Grove to where Petunia Street started. Lupin Street turned off the Grove a bit further down, so his mother would see him across the road, waving and smiling encouragingly, till she'd seen him turn the corner into Lupin Street. Gran's house was about a hundred yards down. That hundred yards was his free time, his alone time.

"Mind you run all the way," his mother called after him.

But at the corner he always stopped running and began to dawdle, stopping to play with the cat that roamed about the bit of waste ground, or climbing on the pile of bricks the builders never came to build into anything. Sometimes, if she wasn't too bad with her arthritis, gran would be waiting for him at her gate, and he didn't mind having to forgo the cat and the climbing because it was so nice in gran's house. Gran had a big T.V. set—unusually big for those days—and he'd watch it, eating chocolate, until his father knocked off at the factory and turned up for tea. Tea was lovely, fish and chips that gran didn't fetch from the shop but cooked herself, cream meringues and chocolate eclairs, tinned peaches with evaporated milk, the lot washed down with fizzy lemonade. ("It's a disgrace the way your mother spoils that boy, Stan.") They were supposed to be home by seven, but every week when it got round to seven, gran would remember there was a cowboy film coming up on T.V. and there'd be cocoa and biscuits and potato crisps to go with it. They'd be lucky to be home in Petunia Street before nine.

"Don't blame me," said his mother, "if his school work suffers next day."

That dreadful evening his mother left him as usual at the corner and saw him across the road. He could remember that, and remember too how he'd looked to see if gran was at her gate. When he'd made sure she wasn't, he'd wandered on to the building site to cajole the cat out of the nest she'd made for herself among the rubble. It was late March, a fine afternoon and still broad daylight at four. He was stroking the cat, thinking how thin and bony she was and how some of gran's fish and chips would do her good, when—what? What next? At this point the curtain came down. Three hours later it lifted, and he was in Plumtree Grove, walking along quite calmly ("Running in terror with that Man after him"), when whom should he meet but Mrs Wilson's Brenda out for the evening with her boy friend. Brenda had pointed at him, stared and shouted. She ran up to him and clutched him and squeezed him till he could hardly breathe. Was that what had frightened him into losing his memory? They said no. They said he'd been frightened before ("Terrified out of his life") and that Brenda's grabbing him and the dreadful shriek his mother gave when she saw him had nothing to do with it.

Petunia Street was full of police cars and there was a crowd outside their house. Brenda hustled him him in, shouting, "I've found him, I've found him!" and there was his father all white in the face, talking to policemen, his mother half dead on the sofa being given brandy, and—wonder of wonders—his gran there too. That had been one of the strangest things of that whole strange evening, that his gran had set foot in their house and his mother hadn't gone out of it.

They all started asking him questions at once. Had he answered them? All that remained in his memory was his mother's scream. That endured, that shattering sound, and the great open mouth from which it issued as she leapt upon him. Somehow, although he couldn't have explained why, he connected that scream and her seizing him as if to swallow him up, with the descent of the curtain.

He was never allowed to be alone after that, not even to play with John in the Wilsons' garden, and he was never allowed to forget those events he couldn't remember. There was no question of going to gran's even under supervision, for gran's arthritis had got so bad they'd put her in the old people's ward at Upfield Hospital. The Man was never found. A couple of years later a little girl from Plumtree Grove got taken away and murdered. They never found that Man either, but his mother was sure they were one and the same.

"And it might have been our Richard. It doesn't bear thinking of, that Man roaming the streets like a wild beast."

"What did he do to me, mum?" asked Richard, trying.

"If you don't remember, so much the better. You want to forget all about it, put it right out of your life."

If only she'd let him. "What did he *do*, dad?"

"I don't know, Rich. None of us knows, me nor the police nor your mum, for all she says. Women like to set themselves up as knowing all about things, but it's my belief you never told her no more than you told us."

She took him to school and fetched him home until he was twelve. The other kids teased him mercilessly. He wasn't allowed to go to their houses or have any of them to his. ("You never know who they know or what sort of connections they've got.") His mother only stopped going everywhere with him when he got taller than she was, and anyone could see he was too big for any Man to attack.

Growing up brought no elucidation of that dreadful evening but it did bring, with adolescence, the knowledge of what might have happened. And as he came to understand that it wasn't only threats and blows and stories of horror which the Man might have inflicted on him, he felt an alien in his own body or as if that body were covered with a slime which nothing could wash away. For there was no way of knowing now, nothing to do about it but wish his mother would leave the subject alone, avoid getting friendly with people, and work hard at school.

He did very well there, for he was naturally intelligent and had no outside diversions. No one was surprised when he got to a good university, not Oxford or Cambridge but nearly as good ("Imagine, all that brainpower might have been wasted if that Man had had his way"), where he began to read for a science degree. He was the first member of his family ever to go to college, and the only cloud in the sky was that his gran, as his father pointed out, wasn't there to see his glory.

She had died in the hospital when he was fourteen and she'd left her house to his parents. They'd sold it and theirs and bought a much nicer, bigger one with a proper garden and a garage in a suburb some five miles further out from Upfield. The little bit of money she'd saved she left to Richard, to come to him when he was eighteen. It was just enough to buy a car, and when he came down from university for the Easter holidays, he bought a two-year-old Ford and took and passed his driving test.

"That boy," said his mother, "passes every exam that comes his way. It's like as if he *couldn't* fail if he tried. But he's got a guardian angel watching over him, has had ever since he was six." Her husband had admonished her for her too-excellent memory and now she referred only obliquely to that dreadful evening. "When you-know-what happened and he was spared."

She watched him drive expertly round the block, her only regret that he hadn't got a nice girl beside him, a sensible, hard-working fiancée—not one of your tarty pieces—saving up for the deposit on a house and good furniture. Richard had never had a girl. There was one at college he liked and who, he thought, might like him. But he didn't ask her out. He was never quite sure whether he was fit for any girl to know, let alone love.

The day after he'd passed his test he thought he'd drive over to Upfield and look up John Wilson. There was more in this, he confessed to himself, than a wish to revive old friendship. John was the only friend he'd really ever had, but he'd always felt inferior to him, for John had been (and had had the chance to be) easy and sociable and had had a girl to go out with when he was only fourteen. He rather liked the idea of arriving outside the Wilsons' house, fresh from his first two terms at university and in his own car.

It was a Wednesday in early April, a fine, mild afternoon and still, of course, broad daylight at four. He chose a Wednesday because that was early closing day in Upfield and John wouldn't be in the hardware shop where he'd worked ever since he left school three years before.

But as he approached Petunia Street up Plumtree Grove from the southerly direction, it struck him that he'd quite like to take a look at his gran's old house and see whether they'd ever built anything on that bit of waste ground. For years and years, half his lifetime, those bricks had lain there, though the thin old cat had disappeared or died long before Richard's parents moved. And the bricks were still there, overgrown now by grass and nettles. He drove into Lupin Street, moving slowly along the pavement edge until he was within sight of his gran's house. There was enough of his mother in him to stop him parking directly outside the house ("Keep yourself to yourself and don't pry into what doesn't concern you"), so he stopped the car some few yards this side of it.

It had been painted a bright pink, the window woodwork picked out in sky-blue. Richard thought he liked it better the way it used to be, cream plaster and brown wood, but he didn't move away. A strange feeling had come over him, stranger than any he could remember having experienced, which kept him where he was, staring at the wilderness of rubble and brick and weeds. Just nostalgia, he thought, just going back to those Wednesdays which had been the high spots of his weeks.

It was funny the way he kept looking among the rubble for the old cat to appear. If she were alive, she'd be as old as he by now and not many cats live that long. But he kept on looking just the same, and presently, as he was trying to pull himself out of this dreamy, dazed feeling and go off to John's, a living creature did appear behind the shrub-high weeds. A boy, about eight. Richard didn't intend to get out of the car. He found himself out of it, locking the door and then strolling over on to the building site.

You couldn't really see much from a car, not details. That must have been why he'd got out, to examine more closely this scene of his childhood pleasures. It seemed very small, not the wild expanse of brick hills and grassy gullies he remembered, but a scrubby little bit of land twenty feet wide and perhaps twice as long. Of course it had seemed bigger because he had been so much smaller, smaller even than this little boy who now sat on a brick mountain, eyeing him.

He didn't mean to speak to the boy, for he wasn't a child any more but a Man. And if there is an explicit rule that a child mustn't speak to strangers, there is an implicit, unstated one, that a Man doesn't speak to children. If he had *meant* to speak, his words would have been very different, something about having played there himself once perhaps, or having lived nearby. The words he did use came to his lips as if they had been placed there by some external (or deeply internal) ruling authority.

"You're trespassing on private land. Did you know that?"

The boy began to ease himself down. "All the kids play here, mister."

"Maybe, but that's no excuse. Where do you live?"

In Petunia Street, but I'm going to my gran's. . . . No.

"Upfield High Road."

"I think you'd better get in my car," the Man said, "and I'll take you home."

Doubtfully, the boy said, "There won't be no one there. My mum works late Wednesdays and I haven't got no dad. I'm to go straight home from school and have my tea and wait for when my mum comes at seven."

Straight to my gran's and have my tea and . . .

"But you haven't, have you? You hung about trespassing on other people's property."

"You a cop, mister?"

"Yes," said the Man, "yes, I am."

The boy got into the car quite willingly. "Are we going to the cop shop?"

"We may go to the police station later. I want to have a talk to you first. We'll go . . ." Where should they go? South London has many open spaces, commons they're called. Wandsworth Common, Tooting Common, Streatham Common. . . . What made him choose Drywood Common, so far away, a place he'd heard of but hadn't visited, so far as he knew, in his life? The Man had known, and he was the Man now, wasn't he? "We'll go to Drywood and have a talk. There's some chocolate on the dashboard shelf. Have a bit if you like." He started the car and they drove off past gran's old house. "Have it all," he said.

The boy had it all. He introduced himself as Barry. He was eight and he had no brothers or sisters or father, just his mum, who worked to keep them both. His mum had told him never to get into strangers' cars, but a cop was different, wasn't it?

"Quite different," said the Man. "Different altogether."

It wasn't easy finding Drywood Common because the signposting was bad around there. But the strange thing was that, once there, the whole lay-out of the common was familiar to him.

"We'll park," he said, "down by the lake."

He found the lake with ease, driving along the main road that bisected the common, then turning left on to a smaller lane. There were ducks on the pond. It was surrounded by trees, but in the distance you could see houses and a little row of shops. He parked the car by the water and switched off the engine.

Barry was very calm and trusting. He listened intelligently to the policeman's lecture on behaving himself and not trespassing, and he didn't fidget or seem bored when the Man stopped talking about that and began to talk about himself. The Man had had a lonely sort of life, a bit like being in prison, and he'd never been allowed out alone. Even when he was in his own room doing his homework, he'd been watched ("Leave your door open, dear. We don't want any secrets in this house"), and he hadn't had a single real friend. Would Barry be his friend, just for a few hours, just for that evening? Barry would.

"But you're grown up now," he said.

The Man nodded. Barry said later when he recalled the details of what his mother called "that nasty experience"—for he was always able to remember every detail—that it was at this point the Man had begun to cry.

A small, rather dirty hand touched the Man's hand and held it. No one had ever held his hand like that before. Not possessively or commandingly ("Hold on to me tight, Richard, while we cross the road") but gently, sympathetically—lovingly? Their hands remained clasped, the small one covering the large, then the large enclosing and gripping the small. A tension, as of time stopped, held the two people in the car still. The boy broke it, and time moved again.

"I'm getting a bit hungry," he said.

"Are you? It's past your teatime. I'll tell you what, we could have some fish and chips. One of those shops over there is a fish and chip shop."

Barry started to get out of the car.

"No, not you," the Man said. "It's better if I go alone. You wait here. O.K.?"

"O.K.," Barry said.

He was only gone ten minutes—for he knew exactly and from a distance which one of the shops it was—and when he got back Barry was waiting for him. The fish and chips were good, almost as good as those gran used to cook. By the time they had finished eating and had wiped their greasy fingers on his handkerchief, dusk had come. Lights were going up in those far-off shops and houses but here, down by the lake, the trees made it quite dark.

"What's the time?" said Barry.

"A quarter past six."

"I ought to be getting back now."

"How about a game of hide and seek first? Your mum won't be home yet. I can get you back to Upfield in ten minutes."

"I don't know. . . . Suppose she gets in early?"

"Please," the Man said. "*Please*, just for a little while. I used to play hide and seek down here when I was a kid."

"But you said you never played anywhere. You said . . ."

"Did I? Maybe I didn't. I'm a bit confused."

Barry looked at him gravely. "I'll hide first," he said.

He watched Barry disappear among the trees. Grown-ups who play hide and seek don't keep to the rules, they don't bother with that counting to a hundred bit. But the Man did. He counted slowly and seriously, and then he got out of the car and began walking round the pond. It took him a long time to find Barry, who was more proficient at this game than he, a proficiency which showed when it was his turn to do the seeking. The darkness was deepening, and there was no one else on the common. He and the boy were quite alone.

Barry had gone to hide. In the car the Man sat counting—ninety-seven, ninety-eight, ninety-nine, one hundred. When he stopped he was aware of the silence of the place, alleviated only by the faint, distant hum of traffic on the South Circular Road, just as the darkness was alleviated by the red blush of the sky, radiating the glow of London. Last time round, it hadn't been this dark. The boy wasn't behind any of the trees or in the bushes by the waterside or covered by the brambles in the ditch that ran parallel to the road.

Where the hell had the stupid kid got to? His anger was irrational, for he had suggested the game himself. Was he angry because the boy had proved better at it than he? Or was it something deeper and fiercer than that, rage at rejection by this puny and ignorant little savage?

"Where are you, Barry? Come on out. I've had about enough of this."

There was no answer. The wind rustled, and a tiny twig scuttered down out of a treetop to his feet. God, that little devil! What'll I do if I can't find him? What the hell's he playing at?

When I find him I'll—I'll kill him.

He shivered. The blood was throbbing in his head. He broke a stick off a bush and began thrashing about with it, enraged, shouting into the dark silence, "Barry, Barry, come out! Come out at once, d'you hear me?" He doesn't want me, he doesn't care about me, no one will ever want me. . . .

Then he heard a giggle from a treetop above him, and suddenly there was a crackling of twigs, a slithering sound. Not quite above him—over there. In the giggle, he thought, there was a note of jeering. But where, where? Down by the water's edge. He'd been up in the tree that almost overhung the pond. There was a thud as small feet bounced on to the ground, and again that maddening, gleeful giggle. For a moment the Man stood still. His hands clenched as on a frail neck, and he held them pressed together, crushing out life. Run, Barry, run. . . . Run, Richard, to Plumtree Grove and Brenda, to home and mother, who knows what dreadful evenings are.

The Man thrust his way through the bushes, making for the pond. The boy would be away by now, but not far away. And his legs were long enough and strong enough to outrun him, his hands strong enough to ensure there would be no future of doubt and fear and curtained memory.

But he was nowhere, nowhere. And yet. . . . What was that sound, as of stealthy, fearful feet creeping away? He wheeled round, and there was the boy coming towards him, walking a little timidly between the straight, grey tree trunks *towards* him. A thick constriction gripped his throat. There must have been something in his face, some threatening gravity made more intense by the half-dark, that stopped the boy in his tracks. Run, Barry, run, run fast away. . . .

They stared at each other for a moment, for a lifetime, for twelve long years. Then the boy gave a merry laugh, fearless and innocent. He ran forward and flung himself into the Man's arms, and the Man, in a great release of pain and anguish, lifted the boy up, lifted him laughing into his own laughing face. They laughed with a kind of rapture at finding each other at last, and in the dark, under the whispering trees, each held the other close in an embrace of warmth and friendship.

"Come on," Richard said, "I'll take you home. I don't know what I was doing, bringing you here in the first place."

"To play hide and seek," said Barry. "We had a nice time."

They got back into the car. It was after seven when they got to Upfield High Road, but not much after.

"I don't reckon my mum's got in yet."

"I'll drop you here. I won't go up to your place." Richard opened the car door to let him out. "Barry?"

"What is it, mister?"

"Don't ever take a lift from a Man again, will you? Promise me?"

Barry nodded. "O.K."

"I once took a lift from a stranger, and for years I couldn't remember what had happened. It sort of came back to me tonight, meeting you. I remember it all now. He was all right, just a bit lonely like me. We had fish and chips on Drywood Common and played hide and seek like you and me, and he brought me back nearly to my house—like I've brought you. But it wouldn't always be like that."

"How do you know?"

Richard looked at his strong young man's hands. "I just know," he said. "Good-bye, Barry, and—thanks."

He drove away, turning once to see that the boy was safely in his house. Barry told his mother all about it, but she insisted it must have been a nasty experience and called the police. Since Barry couldn't remember the number of the car and had no idea of the stranger's name, there was little they could do. They never found the Man.

People Don't Do Such Things

People don't do such things.

That's the last line of *Hedda Gabler,* and Ibsen makes this chap say it out of a sort of bewilderment at finding truth stranger than fiction. I know just how he felt. I say it myself every time I come up against the hard reality that Reeve Baker is serving fifteen years in prison for murdering my wife, and that I played my part in it, and that it happened to us three. People don't do such things. But they do.

Real life had never been stranger than fiction for me. It had always been beautifully pedestrian and calm and pleasant, and all the people I knew jogged along in the same sort of way. Except Reeve, that is. I suppose I made a friend of Reeve and enjoyed his company so much because of the contrast between his manner of living and my own, and so that when he had gone home I could say comfortably to Gwendolen, "How dull our lives must seem to Reeve!"

An acquaintance of mine had given him my name when he had got into a mess with his finances and was having trouble with the Inland Revenue. As an accountant with a good many writers among my clients, I was used to their irresponsible attitude to money—the way they fall back on the excuse of artistic temperament for what is, in fact, calculated tax evasion—and I was able to sort things out for Reeve and show him how to keep more or less solvent. As a way, I suppose, of showing his gratitude, Reeve took Gwendolen and me out to dinner, then we had him over at our place, and after that we became close friends.

Writers and the way they work hold a fascination for ordinary chaps like me. It's a mystery to me where they get their ideas from, apart from constructing the thing and creating character and making their characters talk and so on. But Reeve could do it all right, and set the whole lot at the court of Louis Quinze or in mediaeval Italy or what not. I've read all nine of his historical novels and admired what you might call his virtuosity. But I only read them to please him really. Detective stories were what I preferred and I seldom bothered with any other form of fiction.

Gwendolen once said to me it was amazing Reeve could fill his books with so much drama when he was living drama all the time. You'd imagine he'd have got rid of it all on paper. I think the truth was that every one of his heroes was himself, only transformed into Cesare Borgia or Casanova. You could see Reeve in them all, tall, handsome, and dashing as they were, and each a devil with the women. Reeve had got divorced from his wife a year or so before I'd met him, and since then he'd had a string of girl friends—models, actresses, girls in the fashion trade, secretaries, journalists, schoolteachers, high-powered lady executives, and even a dentist. Once when we were over at his place he played us a record of an aria from *Don Giovanni*—another character Reeve identified with and wrote about. It was called the Catalogue Song and it listed all the types of girls the Don had made love to, blonde, brunette, redhead, young, old, rich, poor, ending up with something about as long as she wears a petticoat you know what he does. Funny, I even remember the Italian for that bit, though it's the only Italian I know. *Purche porti la gonella voi sapete quel che fa.* Then the singer laughed in an unpleasant way, laughed to music with a seducer's sneer, and Reeve laughed too, saying it gave him a fellow-feeling.

I'm old-fashioned, I know that. I'm conventional. Sex for marriage, as far as I'm concerned, and what sex you have before marriage—I never had much—I can't help thinking of as a shameful, secret thing. I never even believed that people did have much of it outside marriage. All talk and boasting, I thought. I really did think that. And I kidded myself that when Reeve talked of going out with a new girl he meant going out with. Taking out for a meal, I thought, and dancing with and taking home in a taxi, and then maybe a good-night kiss on the doorstep. Until one Sunday morning, when Reeve was coming over for lunch, I phoned him to ask if he'd meet us in the pub for a pre-lunch drink. He sounded half asleep and I could hear a girl giggling in the background. Then I heard him say, "Get some clothes on, lovey, and make us a cup of tea, will you? My head's splitting."

I told Gwendolen.

"What did you expect?" she said.

"I don't know," I said. "I thought you'd be shocked."

"He's very good-looking and he's only thirty-seven. It's natural." But she had blushed a little. "I am rather shocked," she said. "We don't belong in his sort of life, do we?"

And yet we remained in it, on the edge of it. As we got to know Reeve better, he put aside those small prevarications he had employed to save our feelings. And he would tell us, without shyness, anecdotes of his amorous past and present. The one about the girl who was so possessive that even though he had broken with her, she had got into his flat in his absence and been lying naked in his bed when he brought his new girl home that night; the one about the married woman who had hidden him for two hours in her wardrobe until her husband had gone out; the girl who had come to borrow a pound of sugar and had stayed all night; fair girls, dark girls, plump, thin, rich, poor. . . . *Purche porti la gonella voi sapete quel che fa.*

"It's another world," said Gwendolen.

And I said, "How the other half lives."

We were given to clichés of this sort. Our life was a cliché, the commonest sort of life led by middle-class people in the Western world. We had a nice detached house in one of the right suburbs, solid furniture, and lifetime-lasting carpets. I had my car and she hers. I left for the once at half past eight and returned at six. Gwendolen cleaned the house and went shopping and gave coffee mornings. In the evenings we liked to sit at home and watch television, generally going to bed at eleven. I think I was a good husband. I never forgot my wife's birthday or failed to send her roses on our anniversary or omitted to do my share of the dishwashing. And she was an excellent wife, romantically inclined, not sensual. At any rate, she was never sensual with me.

She kept every birthday card I ever sent her, and the Valentines I sent her while we were engaged. Gwendolen was one of those women who hoard and cherish small mementoes. In a drawer of her dressing table she kept the menu card from the restaurant where we celebrated our engagement, a picture postcard of the hotel where we spent our honeymoon, every photograph of us that had ever been taken, our wedding pictures in a leather-bound album. Yes, she was an arch-romantic, and in her diffident way, with an air of daring, she would sometimes reproach Reeve for his callousness.

"But you can't do that to someone who loves you," she said when he had announced his brutal intention of going off on holiday without telling his latest girl friend where he was going or even that he was going at all. "You'll break her heart."

"Gwendolen, my love, she hasn't got a heart. Women don't have them. She has another sort of machine, a combination of telescope, lie detector, scalpel, and castrating device."

"You're too cynical," said my wife. "You may fall in love yourself one day and then you'll know how it feels."

"Not necessarily. As Shaw said"—Reeve was always quoting what other writers had said—"'Don't do unto others as you would have others do unto you, as we don't all have the same tastes.'"

"We all have the same taste about not wanting to be ill-treated."

"She should have thought of that before she tried to control my life. No, I shall quietly disappear for a while. I mightn't go away, in fact. I might just say I'm going away and lie low at home for a fortnight. Fill up the deep freeze, you know, and lay in a stock of liquor. I've done it before in this sort of situation. It's rather pleasant and I get a hell of a lot of work done."

Gwendolen was silenced by this and, I must say, so was I. You may wonder, after these examples of his morality, just what it was I saw in Reeve. It's hard now for me to remember. Charm, perhaps, and a never-failing hospitality; a rueful way of talking about his own life as if it was all he could hope for, while mine was the ideal all men would aspire to; a helplessness about his financial affairs combined with an admiration for my grasp of them; a manner of talking to me as if we were equally men of the world, only I had chosen the better part. When invited to one of our dull, modest gatherings, he would always be the exciting friend with the witty small talk, the reviver of a failing party, the industrious barman; above all, the one among our friends who wasn't an accountant, a bank manager, a solicitor, a general practitioner, or a company executive. We had his books on our shelves. Our friends borrowed them and told their friends they'd met Reeve Baker at our house. He gave us a cachet that raised us enough centimetres above the level of the bourgeoisie to make us interesting.

Perhaps, in those days, I should have asked myself what it was he saw in us.

It was about a year ago that I first sensed a coolness between Gwendolen and Reeve. The banter they had gone in for, which had consisted in wry confessions or flirtatious compliments from him, and shy, somewhat maternal reproofs from her, stopped almost entirely. When we all three were together they talked to each other through me, as if I were their interpreter. I asked Gwendolen if he'd done something to upset her.

She looked extremely taken aback. "What makes you ask?"

"You always seem a bit peeved with him."

"I'm sorry," she said. "I'll try to be nicer. I didn't know I'd changed."

She had changed to me too. She flinched sometimes when I touched her, and although she never refused me, there was an apathy about her love-making.

"What's the matter?" I asked her after a failure which disturbed me because it was so unprecedented.

She said it was nothing, and then: "We're getting older. You can't expect things to be the same as when we were first married."

"For God's sake," I said, "you're thirty-five and I'm thirty-nine. We're not in our dotage."

She sighed and looked unhappy. She had become moody and difficult. Although she hardly opened her mouth in Reeve's presence, she talked about him a lot when he wasn't there, seizing upon almost any excuse to discuss him and speculate about his character. And she seemed inexplicably annoyed when, on our tenth wedding anniversary, a greetings card arrived addressed to us both from him. I, of course, had sent her roses. At the end of that week I missed a receipt for a bill I'd paid—as an accountant, I'm naturally circumspect about these things—and I searched through our wastepaper basket, thinking I might have thrown it away. I found it, and I also found the anniversary card I'd sent Gwendolen to accompany the roses.

All these things I noticed. That was the trouble with me—I noticed things but I lacked the experience of life to add them up and make a significant total. I didn't have the worldly wisdom to guess why my wife was always out when I phoned her in the afternoons, or why she was for ever buying new clothes. I noticed, I wondered, that was all.

I noticed things about Reeve too. For one thing, that he'd stopped talking about his girl friends.

"He's growing up at last," I said to Gwendolen.

She reacted with warmth, with enthusiasm. "I really think he is."

But she was wrong. He had only three months of what I thought of as celibacy. And then when he talked of a new girl friend, it was to me alone. Confidentially, over a Friday-night drink in the pub, he told me of this "marvellous chick," twenty years old, he had met at a party the week before.

"It won't last, Reeve," I said.

"I sincerely hope not. Who wants it to *last?*"

Not Gwendolen, certainly. When I told her, she was incredulous, then aghast. And when I said I was sorry I'd told her since Reeve's backsliding upset her so much, she snapped at me that she didn't want to discuss him. She became even more snappy and nervous and depressed too. Whenever the phone rang she jumped. Once or twice I came home to find no wife, no dinner prepared; then she'd come in, looking haggard, to say she'd been out for a walk. I got her to see our doctor and he put her on tranquillisers, which just made her more depressed.

I hadn't seen Reeve for ages. Then, out of the blue, he phoned me at work to say he was off to the South of France for three weeks.

"In your state of financial health?" I said. I'd had a struggle getting him to pay the January instalment of his twice-yearly income tax, and I knew he was practically broke till he got the advance on his new book in May. "The South of France is a bit pricey, isn't it?"

"I'll manage," he said. "My bank manager's one of my fans and he's let me have an overdraft."

Gwendolen didn't seem very surprised to hear about Reeve's holiday. He'd told me he was going on his own—the "marvellous chick" had long disappeared—and she said she thought he needed the rest, especially as there wouldn't be any of those girls to bother him, as she put it.

When I first met Reeve he'd been renting a flat but I persuaded him to buy one, for security and as an investment. The place was known euphemistically as a garden flat but it was in fact a basement, the lower ground floor of a big Victorian house in Bayswater. My usual route to work didn't take me along his street, but sometimes when the traffic was heavy I'd go through the back doubles and past his house. After he'd been away for about two weeks I happened to do this one morning and, of course, I glanced at Reeve's window. One always does glance at a friend's house, I think, when one is passing even if one knows that friend isn't at home. His bedroom was at the front, the top half of the window visible, the lower half concealed by the rise of lawn. I noticed that the curtains were drawn. Not particularly wise, I thought, an invitation to burglars, and then I forgot about it. But two mornings later I passed that way again, passed very slowly this time as there was a traffic hold-up, and again I glanced at Reeve's window.

The curtains were no longer quite drawn. There was a gap about six inches wide between them. Now, whatever a burglar may do, it's very unlikely he'll pull back drawn curtains. I didn't consider burglars this time. I thought Reeve must have come back early.

Telling myself I should be late for work anyway if I struggled along in this traffic jam, I parked the car as soon as I could at a meter. I'll knock on old Reeve's door, I thought, and get him to make me a cup of coffee. There was no answer. But as I looked once more at that window I was almost certain those curtains had been moved again, and in the past ten minutes. I rang the doorbell of the woman in the flat upstairs. She came down in her dressing gown.

"Sorry to disturb you," I said. "But do you happen to know if Mr. Baker's come back?"

"He's not coming back till Saturday," she said.

"Sure of that?"

"Of course I'm sure," she said rather huffily. "I put a note through his door Monday, and if he was back he'd have come straight up for this parcel I took in for him."

"Did he take his car, d'you know?" I said, feeling like a detective in one of my favourite crime novels.

"Of course he did. What is this? What's he done?"

I said he'd done nothing, as far as I knew, and she banged the door in my face. So I went down the road to the row of lock-up garages. I couldn't see much through the little panes of frosted glass in the door of Reeve's garage, just enough to be certain the interior wasn't empty but that that greenish blur was the body of Reeve's Fiat. And then I knew for sure. He hadn't gone away at all. I chuckled to myself as I imagined him lying low for these three weeks in his flat, living off food from the deep freeze and spending most of his time in the back regions where, enclosed as those rooms were by a courtyard with high walls, he could show lights day and night with impunity. Just wait till Saturday, I thought, and I pictured myself asking him for details of his holiday, laying little traps for him, until even he with his writer's powers of invention would have to admit he'd never been away at all.

Gwendolen was laying the table for our evening meal when I got in. She, I'd decided, was the only person with whom I'd share this joke. I got all her attention the minute I mentioned Reeve's name, but when I reached the bit about his car being in his garage she stared at me and all the colour went out of her face. She sat down, letting the bunch of knives and forks she was holding fall into her lap.

"What on earth's the matter?" I said.

"How could he be so cruel? How could he do that to anyone?"

"Oh, my dear, Reeve's quite ruthless where women are concerned. You remember, he told us he'd done it before."

"I'm going to phone him," she said, and I saw that she was shivering. She dialled his number and I heard the ringing tone start.

"He won't answer," I said. "I wouldn't have told you if I'd thought it was going to upset you."

She didn't say any more. There were things cooking on the stove and the table was half laid, but she left all that and went into the hall. Almost immediately afterwards I heard the front door close.

I know I'm slow on the uptake in some ways but I'm not stupid. Even a husband who trusts his wife like I trusted mine—or, rather, never considered there was any need for trust—would know, after that, that something had been going on. Nothing much, though, I told myself. A crush perhaps on her part, hero-worship which his flattery and his confidences had fanned. Naturally, she'd feel let down, betrayed, when she discovered he'd deceived her as to his whereabouts when he'd led her to believe she was a special friend and privy to all his secrets. But I went upstairs just the same to reassure myself by looking in that dressing-table drawer where she kept her souvenirs. Dishonourable? I don't think so. She had never locked it or tried to keep its contents private from me.

And all those little mementoes of our first meeting, our courtship, our marriage were still there. Between a birthday card and a Valentine I saw a pressed rose. But there too, alone in a nest made out of a lace handkerchief I had given her, were a locket and a button. The locket was one her mother had left to her, but the photograph in it, that of some long-dead unidentifiable relative, had been replaced by a cut-out of Reeve from a snapshot. On the reverse side was a lock of hair. The button I recognised as coming from Reeve's blazer, though it hadn't, I noticed, been cut off. He must have lost it in our house and she'd picked it up. The hair was Reeve's, black, wavy, here and there with a thread of grey, but again it hadn't been cut off. On one of our visits to his flat she must have combed it out of his hairbrush and twisted it into a lock. Poor little Gwendolen. . . . Briefly, I'd suspected Reeve. For one dreadful moment, sitting down there after she'd gone out, I'd asked myself, could he have . . . ? Could my best friend have . . . ? But no. He hadn't even sent her a letter or a flower. It had been all on her side, and for that reason—I knew where she was bound for—I must stop her reaching him and humiliating herself.

I slipped the things into my pocket with some vague idea of using them to show her how childish she was being. She hadn't taken her car. Gwendolen always disliked driving in Central London. I took mine and drove to the tube station I knew she'd go to.

She came out a quarter of an hour after I got there, walking fast and glancing nervously to the right and left of her. When she saw me she gave a little gasp and stood stock-still.

"Get in, darling," I said gently. "I want to talk to you."

She got in but she didn't speak. I drove down to the Bayswater Road and into the Park. There, on the Ring, I parked under the plane trees, and because she still didn't utter a word, I said, "You mustn't think I don't understand. We've been married ten years and I daresay I'm a dull sort of chap. Reeve's exciting and different and—well, maybe it's only natural for you to think you've fallen for him."

She stared at me stonily. "I love him and he loves me."

"That's nonsense," I said, but it wasn't the chill of the spring evening that made me shiver. "Just because he's used that charm of his on you . . ."

She interrupted me. "I want a divorce."

"For heaven's sake," I said, "you hardly know Reeve. You've never been alone with him, have you?"

"Never been alone with him?" She gave a brittle, desperate laugh. "He's been my lover for six months. And now I'm going to him. I'm going to tell him he doesn't have to hide from women any more because I'll be with him all the time."

In the half-dark I gaped at her. "I don't believe you," I said, but I did. I did. "You mean you along with all the rest . . . ? My wife?"

"I'm going to be Reeve's wife. I'm the only one that understands him, the only one he can talk to. He told me that just before—before he went away."

"Only he didn't go away." There was a great redness in front of my eyes like a lake of blood. "You fool," I shouted at her. "Don't you see it's you he's hiding from, *you*? He's done this to get away from you like he's got away from all the others. Love you? He never even gave you a present, not even a photograph. If you go there, he won't let you in. You're the last person he'd let in."

"I'm going to him," she cried, and she began to struggle with the car door. "I'm going to him, to live with him, and I never want to see you again!"

In the end I drove home alone. Her wish came true and she never did see me again.

When she wasn't back by eleven I called the police. They asked me to go down to the police station and fill out a Missing Persons form, but they didn't take my fear very seriously. Apparently when a woman of Gwendolen's age disappears they take it for granted she's gone off with a man. They took it seriously all right when a park keeper found her strangled body among some bushes in the morning.

That was on the Thursday. The police wanted to know where Gwendolen could have been going so far from her home. They wanted the names and addresses of all our friends. Was there anyone we knew in Kensington or Paddington or Bayswater, anywhere in the vicinity of the Park? I said there was no one. The next day they asked me again and I said, as if I'd just remembered, "Only Reeve Baker. The novelist, you know." I gave them his address. "But he's away on holiday, has been for three weeks. He's not coming home till tomorrow."

What happened after that I know from the evidence given at Reeve's trial, his trial for the murder of my wife. The police called on him on Saturday morning. I don't think they suspected him at all at first. My reading of crime fiction has taught me they would have asked him for any information he could give about our private life.

Unfortunately for him, they had already talked to some of his neighbours. Reeve had led all these people to think he had really gone away. The milkman and the paper boy were both certain he had been away. So when the police questioned him about that, and he knew just why they were questioning him, he got into a panic. He didn't dare say he'd been in France. They could have shown that to be false without the least trouble. Instead, he told the truth and said he'd been lying low to escape the attentions of a woman. Which woman? He wouldn't say, but the woman in the flat upstairs would. Time and time again she had seen Gwendolen visit him in the afternoons, had heard them quarrelling, Gwendolen protesting her love for him and he shouting that he wouldn't be controlled, that he'd do anything to escape her possessiveness.

He had, of course, no alibi for the Wednesday night. But the judge and the jury could see he'd done his best to arrange one. Novelists are apt to let their imaginations run away with them; they don't realise how astute and thorough the police are. And there was firmer evidence of his guilt even than that. Three main exhibits were produced in the court: Reeve's blazer with a button missing from the sleeve; that very button; a cluster of his hairs. The button had been found beside Gwendolen's body and the hairs on her coat. . . .

My reading of detective stories hadn't been in vain, though I haven't read one since then. People don't, I suppose, after a thing like that.

A Bad Heart

They had been very pressing and at last, on the third time of asking, he had accepted. Resignedly, almost fatalistically, he had agreed to dine with them. But as he began the long drive out of London, he thought petulantly that they ought to have had the tact to drop the acquaintance altogether. No other employee he had sacked had ever made such approaches to him. Threats, yes. Several had threatened him and one had tried blackmail, but no one had ever had the effrontery to invite him to dinner. It wasn't done. A discreet man wouldn't have done it. But of course Hugo Crouch wasn't a discreet man and that, among other things, was why he had been sacked.

He knew why they had asked him. They wanted to hold a court of enquiry, to have the whole thing out. Knowing this, he had suggested they meet in a restaurant and at his expense. They couldn't harangue a man in a public restaurant and he wouldn't be at their mercy. But they had insisted he come to their house and in the end he had given way. He was an elderly man with a heart condition; it was sixteen miles slow driving from his flat to their house—monstrous on a filthy February night—but he would show them he could take it, he would be one too many for them. The chairman of Frasers would show them he wasn't to be intimidated by a bumptious do-gooder like Hugo Crouch, and he would cope with the situation just as he had coped in the past with the blackmailer.

By the time he reached the outskirts of the Forest, the rain was coming down so hard that he had to put his windscreen wipers on to top speed, and he felt more than ever thankful that he had got this new car with all its efficient gadgets. Certainly the firm wouldn't have been able to run to it if he had kept Hugo Crouch on a day longer. If he had agreed to all Hugo's demands, he would still be stuck with that old Daimler and he would never have managed that winter cruise. Hugo had been a real thorn in his flesh what with his extravagance and his choosing to live in a house in the middle of Epping

Forest. And it was in the middle, totally isolated, not even on the edge of one of the Forest villages. The general manager of Frasers had to be within reach, on call. Burying oneself out here was ridiculous.

The car's powerful headlights showed a dark, winding lane ahead, the grey tree trunks making it appear like some sombre, pillared corridor. And this picture was cut off every few seconds by a curtain of rain, to reappear with the sweep of the wipers. Fortunately, he had been there once before, otherwise he might have passed the high brick wall and the wooden gates behind which stood the Crouch house, the peak-roofed Victorian villa, drab, shabby, and to his eyes quite hideous. Anyone who put a demolition order on that would be doing a service to the environment, he thought, and then he drove in through the gates.

There wasn't a single light showing. He remembered that they lived in the back, but they might have put a light on to greet him. But for his car headlamps, he wouldn't have been able to see his way at all. Clutching the box of peppermint creams he had bought for Elizabeth Crouch, he splashed across the almost flooded paving, under eaves from which water poured as from a row of taps, and made for the front door, which happened to be—which *would* be—at the far side of the house. It was hard to tell where their garden ended and the Forest began, for no demarcation was visible. Nothing was visible but black, rain-lashed branches, faintly illuminated by a dim glow showing through the fanlight over the door.

He rang the bell hard, keeping his finger on the push, hoping the rain hadn't got through his coat to his hundred-guinea suit. A jet of water struck the back of his neck, sending a shiver right through him, and then the door was opened.

"Duncan! You must be soaked. Have you had a dreadful journey?"

He gasped out, "Awful, awful!" and ducked into the dry sanctuary of the hall. "What a night!" He thrust the chocolates at her, gave her his hand. Then he remembered that in the old days they always used to kiss. Well, he never minded kissing a pretty woman and it hadn't been her fault. "How are you, Elizabeth?" he said after their cheeks had touched.

"I'm fine. Let me take your coat. I'll take it into the kitchen and dry it. Hugo's in the sitting room. You know your way, don't you?"

Down a long passage, he remembered, that was never properly lighted and wasn't heated at all. The whole place cried out for central heating. He was by now extremely cold and he couldn't help thinking of his flat, where the radiators got so hot that you had to open the windows even in February and where, had he been at home, his housekeeper would at this moment be placing before him a portion of hot paté to be followed by poulet San Josef. Elizabeth Crouch, he recalled, was rather a poor cook.

Outside the sitting-room door he paused, girding himself for the encounter. He hadn't set eyes on Hugo Crouch since the man had marched out of the office in a huff because he, Duncan Fraser, chairman of Frasers, had tentatively suggested he might be happier in another job. Well, the sooner the first words were over the better. Very few men in his position, he thought, would let the matter weigh on their minds at all or have his sensitivity. Very few, for that matter, would have come.

He would be genial, casual, perhaps a little avuncular. Above all, he would avoid at any cost the subject of Hugo's dismissal. They wouldn't be able to make him talk about it if he was determined not to; ultimately, the politeness of hosts to guest would put up a barrier to stop them. He opened the door, smiling pleasantly, achieving a merry twinkle in his eye. "Well, here I am, Hugo! I've made it."

Hugo wore a very sour look, the kind of look Duncan had often seen on his face when some more than usually extravagant order or request of his had been countermanded. He didn't smile. He gave Duncan his hand gravely and asked him what he would like to drink.

Duncan looked quickly around the room, which hadn't changed and was still furnished with rather grim Victorian pieces. There was, at any rate, a huge fire of logs burning in the grate. "Ah, yes, a drink," he said, rubbing his hands together. He didn't dare ask for whisky, which he would have liked best, because his doctor had forbidden it. "A little dry Vermouth?"

"I'm afraid I don't have any Vermouth."

This rejoinder, though spoken quite lightly, though he had even expected something of the sort, gave Duncan a slight shock. It put him on his mettle and yet it jolted him. He had known, of course, that they would start on him but he hadn't anticipated the first move coming so promptly. All right, let the man remind him he couldn't afford fancy drinks because he had lost his job. He, Duncan, wouldn't be drawn. "Sherry, then," he said. "You do have sherry?"

"Oh, yes, we have sherry. Come and sit by the fire."

As soon as he was seated in front of those blazing logs and had begun to thaw out, he decided to pursue the conversation along the lines of the weather. It was the only subject he could think of to break the ice until Elizabeth came in, and they were doing quite well at it, moving into such sidelines as floods in East Anglia and crashes in motorway fog, when she appeared and sat next to him.

"We haven't asked anyone else, Duncan. We wanted to have you to ourselves."

A pointless remark, he thought, under the circumstances. Naturally, they hadn't asked anyone else. The presence of other guests would have defeated the exercise. But perhaps it hadn't been so pointless, after all. It could be an opening gambit.

"Delightful," he said.

"We've got such a lot to talk about. I thought it would be nicer this way."

"Much nicer." Such a lot to talk about? There was only one thing she could mean by that. But she needn't think—silent Hugo sitting there with his grim, moody face needn't think—that he would help them along an inch of the way. If they were going to get on to the subject they would have to do all the spadework themselves. "We were just saying," he said, "how tragic all these motorway crashes are. Now I feel all this could be stopped by a very simple method."

He outlined the simple method but he could tell they weren't really interested and he wasn't surprised when Elizabeth said, "That's fascinating, Duncan, but let's talk about you. What have you been doing lately?"

Controlling the business your husband nearly ruined. "Oh, this and that," he said. "Nothing much."

"Did you go on a cruise this winter?"

"Er—yes, yes I did. The Caribbean, as a matter of fact."

"That's nice. I'm sure the change did you good."

Implying he needed having good done to him, of course. She had only got on to cruises so that she could point out that some people couldn't afford them. "I had a real rest," he said heartily. "I must just tell you about a most amusing thing that happened to me on the way home." He told them but it didn't sound very amusing, and although Elizabeth smiled half-heartedly, Hugo didn't. "Well, it seemed funny at the time," he said.

"We can eat in five minutes," said Elizabeth. "Tell me, Duncan, did you buy that villa you were so keen on in the South of France?"

"Oh, yes, I bought it." She was looking at him very curiously, very impertinently really, waiting for him to apologise for spending his own money, he supposed. "Listen to that rain," he said. "It hasn't let up at all."

They agreed that it hadn't and silence fell. He could tell from the glance they exchanged—he was very astute in these matters—that they knew they had been baulked for the time being. And they both looked pretty fed up, he thought triumphantly. But the woman was weighing in again and a bit nearer the bone this time.

"Who do you think we ran into last week, Duncan? John Churchouse."

The man who had done that printing for Frasers a couple of years back. He had got the order, Duncan remembered, just about the time of Hugo's promotion. He sat tight, drank the last of his sherry.

"He told us he'd been in hospital for months and lost quite a lot of business. I felt so . . ."

"I wonder if I might wash my hands," Duncan asked firmly. "If you could just tell me where the bathroom is?"

"Of course." She looked disappointed, as well she might. "It's the door facing you at the top of the stairs."

Duncan made his way to the bathroom. He mustn't think he was going to get off the hook as easily as that. They would be bound to start on him again during the meal. Very likely they thought a dinner table a good place to hold an inquest. Still, he'd be ready for them, he'd done rather well up to now.

They were both waiting for him at the foot of the stairs to lead him into the dining room and again he saw the woman give her husband one of those looks that are the equivalent of prompting nudges. Hugo was probably getting cold feet. In these cases, of course, it was always the women who were more aggressive. Duncan gave a swift glance at the table and the plate of hors d'oeuvres, sardines and anchovies and artichoke hearts, most unsuitable for the time of year.

"I'm afraid you've been to a great deal of trouble, Elizabeth," he said graciously.

She gave him a dazzling smile. He had forgotten that smile of hers, how it lit her whole face, her eyes as flashing blue as a kingfisher's plumage. "'The labour we delight in,'" she said, "'physics pain.'"

"Ah, *Macbeth*." Good, an excellent topic to get them through the first course. "Do you know, the only time we three ever went to the theatre together was to see *Macbeth*?"

"I remember," she said. "Bread, Duncan?"

"Thank you. I saw a splendid performance of *Macbeth* by that Polish company last week. Perhaps you've seen it?"

"We haven't been to the theatre at all this winter," said Hugo.

She must have kicked him under the table to prompt that one. Duncan took no notice. He told them in detail about the

Polish *Macbeth*, although such was his mounting tenseness that he couldn't remember half the names of the characters or, for that matter, the names of the actors.

"I wish Keith could have seen it," she said. "It's his set play for his exam."

She was going to force him to ask after her sons and be told they had had to take them away from that absurdly expensive boarding school. Well, he wouldn't. Rude it might be, but he wouldn't ask.

"I don't think you ever met our children, Duncan?"

"No, I didn't."

"They'll be home on half-term next week. I'm so delighted that their half-term happens to coincide with mine."

"Yours?" he said suspiciously.

"Elizabeth has gone back to teaching."

"Really?" said Duncan. "No, I won't have any more, thank you. That was delicious. Let me give you a hand. If I could carry something . . . ?"

"Please don't trouble. I can manage." She looked rather offended. "If you two will excuse me I'll see to our main course."

He was left alone with Hugo in the chilly dining room. He shifted his legs from under the cloth to bring them closer to the one-bar electric heater. Hugo began to struggle with the cork of the wine bottle. Unable to extract it, he cursed under his breath.

"Let me try."

"I'll be able to cope quite well, thanks, if you don't watch me," said Hugo sharply, and then, irrelevantly if you didn't know nothing those two said was irrelevant, "I'm doing a course in accountancy."

"As a wine waiter, Hugo," said Duncan, "you make a very good accountant, ha ha!"

Hugo didn't laugh. He got the cork out at last. "I think I'll do all right. I was always reasonably good at figures."

"So you were, so you were. And more than reasonably good." That was true. It had been with personnel that the man was so abysmally bad, giving junior executives and little typists ideas above their station. "I'm sure you'll do well." Why didn't the woman come back? It must have been ten minutes since she had gone off to that kitchen, down those miles of passages. His own wife, long dead, would have got that main course into serving dishes before they had sat down to the hors d'oeuvres. "Get a qualification, that's the thing," he said. In the distance he heard the wheels of a trolley coming. It was a more welcome sound than that of the wheels of the train one has awaited for an hour on a cold platform. He didn't like the woman but anything was better than being alone with Hugo. Why not get it over now, he thought, before they began on the amazingly small roasted chicken which had appeared? He managed a smile. He said, "I can tell you've both fallen on your feet. I'm quite sure, Hugo, you'll look back on all this when you're a successful accountant and thank God you and Frasers parted company."

And that ought to be that. They had put him through their inquisition and now perhaps they would let him eat this overcooked mess that passed for dinner in peace. At last they would talk of something else, not leave it to him who had been making the running all the evening.

But instead of conversation, there was a deep silence. No one seemed to have anything to say. And although Duncan, working manfully at his chicken wing, racked his brains for a topic, he could think of nothing. Their house, his flat, the workpeople at Frasers, his car, the cost of living, her job, Hugo's course, Christmas past, summer to come, all these subjects must inevitably lead by a direct route back to Hugo's dismissal. And Duncan saw with irritable despair that *all* subjects would lead to it because he was he and they were they and the dismissal lay between them like an unavoidable spectre at their dismal feast. From time to time he lifted his eyes from his plate, hoping that she would respond to that famous smile of his, that smile that was growing stiff with insincere use, but each time he looked at her he saw that she was staring fixedly at him, eating hardly anything, her expression concentrated, dispassionate, and somehow dogged. And her eyes had lost their kingfisher flash. They were dull and dead like smoky glass.

So they hadn't had enough then, she and her subdued, morose husband? They wanted to see him abject, not merely referring with open frankness to the dismissal as he had done, but explaining it, apologising. Well, they should have his explanation. There was no escape. Carefully, he placed his knife and fork side by side on his empty plate. Precisely, but very politely, he refused his hostess's offer of more. He took a deep breath as he often did at the beginning of a board meeting, as he had so very often done at those board meetings when Hugo Crouch pressed insistently for staff rises.

"My dear Elizabeth," he began, "my dear Hugo, I know why you asked me here tonight and what you've been hinting at ever since I arrived. And because I want to enjoy your very delightful company without any more awkwardness, I'm going to do here and now what you very obviously want me to do—that is, explain just how it happened that I suggested Hugo would be happier away from Frasers."

Elizabeth said, "Now, Duncan, listen . . ."

"You can say your piece in a moment, Elizabeth. Perhaps you'll be surprised when I say *I am entirely to blame for what happened.* Yes, I admit it, the fault was all mine." He lifted one hand to silence Hugo who was shaking his head vehemently. "No, Hugo, let me finish. As I said, the fault was mine. I made an error of judgment. Oh, yes, I did. I should have been a better judge of men. I should have been able to see when I promoted you that you weren't up to the job. I blame myself for not understanding—well, your limitations."

They were silent. They didn't look at him or at each other.

"We men in responsible positions," he said, "are to blame when the men we appoint can't rise to the heights we envisage for them. We lack vision, that's all. I take the whole burden of it on my shoulders, you see. So shall we forgive and forget?"

He had seldom seen people look so embarrassed, so shamefaced. It just went to show that they were no match for him. His statement had been the last thing they had expected and it was unanswerable. He handed her his plate with its little graveyard of chicken bones among the potato skins and as she took it he saw a look of baulked fury cross her face.

"Well, Elizabeth," he said, unable to resist, "am I forgiven?"

"It's too late now. It's past," she said in a very cold, stony voice. "It's too late for any of this."

"I'm sorry if I haven't given you the explanation you wanted, my dear. I've simply told you the truth."

She didn't say any more. Hugo didn't say anything. And suddenly Duncan felt most uncomfortable. Their condemnatory faces, the way they both seemed to shrink away from him, was almost too much for him. His heart began to pound and he had to tell himself that a racing heart meant nothing, that it was pain and not palpitations he must fear. He reached for one of his little white pills ostentatiously, hoping they would notice what they had done to him.

When still they didn't speak, he said, "I think perhaps I should go now."

"But you haven't had coffee," said Elizabeth.

"Just the same, it might be better . . ."

"Please stay and have coffee," she said firmly, almost sternly, and then she forced a smile. "I insist."

Back in the sitting room they offered him brandy. He refused it because he had to drive home, and the sooner he could begin that drive the happier he would be. Hugo had a large brandy, which he drank at a gulp, the way brandy should never be drunk unless one had had a shock or were steeling oneself for something. Elizabeth had picked up the evening paper and was talking in a very artificial way about a murder case which appeared on the front page.

"I really must go," said Duncan.

"Have some more coffee? It's not ten yet."

Why did they want him to stay? Or, rather, why did she? Hugo was once more busy with the brandy bottle. He would have thought his company must be as tiresome to them as theirs was to him. They had got what they wanted, hadn't they? He drank his second cup of coffee so quickly that it scalded his mouth and then he got up.

"I'll get an umbrella. I'll come out with you," said Hugo.

"Thank you." It was over. He was going to make his escape and he need never see them again. And suddenly he felt that he wouldn't be able to get out of that house fast enough. Really, since he had made his little speech, the atmosphere had been thoroughly disagreeable. "Good night, Elizabeth," he said. What platitudes could he think of that weren't too ludicrous? "Thank you for the meal. Perhaps we may meet again some day."

"I hope we shall and soon, Duncan," she said, but she didn't give him her cheek. Through the open door the rain was driving in against her long skirt. She stood there, watching him go out with Hugo, letting the light pour out to guide them round the corner of the house.

As soon as he was round that corner, Duncan felt an unpleasant jerk of shock. His car lights were blazing, full on.

"How did I come to do a thing like that?"

"I suppose you left them on to see your way to the door," said Hugo, "and then forgot them."

"I'm sure I did *not*."

"You must have. Hold the umbrella and I'll try the ignition." Leaving Duncan on the flooded path under the inadequate umbrella, Hugo got into the driving seat and inserted the ignition key. Duncan watched him, stamping his feet impatiently. "Not a spark," said Hugo. "Your battery's flat."

"It *can't* be."

"I'm afraid it is. Try for yourself."

Duncan tried, getting very wet in the process.

"We'd better go back in the house. We'll get soaked out here."

"What's the matter?" said Elizabeth, who was still standing in the doorway.

"His battery's flat. The car won't start."

Of course it wasn't their fault but somehow Duncan felt it was. It had happened, after all, at their house, to which they had fetched him for a disgraceful purpose. He didn't bother to soften his annoyance. "I'm afraid I'll just have to borrow your car, Hugo."

Elizabeth closed the door. "We don't have a car any more. We couldn't afford to run it. It was either keeping a car or taking the boys away from school, so we sold it."

"I see. Then if I might just use your phone, I'll ring for a hire car. I've a mini-cab number in my wallet." One look at her face told him that wasn't going to be possible either. "Now you'll say you've had the phone cut off." Damn her! Damn them both!

"We could have afforded it, of course. We just didn't need it any more. I'm sorry, Duncan, I just don't know what you can do. But we may as well all go and sit down where it's warmer."

"I don't want to sit down," Duncan almost shouted. "I have to get home." He shook off the hand she had laid on his arm and which seemed to be forcibly detaining him. "I must just walk to the nearest house *with* a phone."

Hugo opened the door. The rain was more like a wall of water than a series of falling drops. "In this?"

"Then what am I supposed to do?" Duncan cried fretfully.

"Stay the night," said Elizabeth calmly. "I really don't know what you can do but stay the night."

The bed was just what he would have expected a bed in the Crouch menage to be—hard, narrow, and cold. She had given him a hot-water bottle, which was an object he hadn't set eyes on in ten years. And Hugo had lent him a pair of pyjamas. All the time this was going on, he had protested that he couldn't stay, that there must be some other way, but in the end he had yielded. Not that they had been welcoming. They had treated the whole thing rather as if—well, how had they treated it? Duncan lay in the dark, clutching the bottle between his knees, and tried to assess just what their attitude had been. Fatalistic, he thought, that was it. They had behaved as if this were inevitable, that there was no escape for him, and here, like it or not, he must stay.

Escape was a ridiculous word, of course, but it was the sort of word you used when you were trapped somewhere for a whole night in the home of people who were obviously antagonistic, if not hostile. Why had he been such a fool as to leave those car lights on? He couldn't remember that he had done and yet he must have. Nobody else would have turned them on. Why should they?

He wished they would go to bed too. That they hadn't he could tell by the light, the rectangular outline of dazzlement, that showed round the frame of his bedroom door. And he could hear them talking, not the words but the buzz of conversation. These late Victorian houses were atrociously built, of course. You could hear every sound. The rain drumming on the roof sounded as if it were pounding on cardboard rather than on slates. He didn't think there was much prospect of sleep. How could he sleep with the noise and all that on his mind, the worry of getting the car moved, of finding some way of getting to the office? And it made him feel very uneasy their staying up like that, particularly as she had said, "If you'll go into the bathroom first, Duncan, we'll follow you." Follow him! That must have been all of half an hour ago. He pressed the switch of his bedlamp and saw that it was eleven-thirty. Time they were in bed if she had to get to her school in the morning and he to his accountancy course.

Once more in the dark, but for that gold-edged rectangle, he considered the car lights question again. He was certain he had turned them out. Of course it was hard to be certain of anything when you were as upset as he. The pressure they had put on him had been simply horrible and the worst moments those when he had been alone with Hugo while that woman was fishing the ancient pullet she'd dished up to him out of her oven. Really, she had been a hell of a time getting that main course when you considered what it had amounted to. Could she . . . ? Only a madwoman would do such a thing and what possible motive could she have had? But if you lived in a remote place and you wanted someone to stay in your house overnight, if you wanted to *keep* him there, how better than to immobilise his car? He shivered, even while he told himself such fancies were absurd.

At any rate, they were coming up now. Every board in the house creaked and the stairs played a tune like a broken old violin. He heard Hugo mumble something—the man had drunk far too much brandy—and then she said, "Leave all the rest to me."

Another shiver that hadn't very much to do with the cold ran through him. He couldn't think why it had. Surely, that was quite a natural thing for a woman to say on going to bed? She only meant, You go to bed and I'll lock up and turn off the lights. He had often said it when his wife was alive. And yet it was a phrase that was familiar to him in quite another context. Turning on his side away from the light and into fresh caverns of icy sheet, he tried to think where he had heard it. A quotation? Yes, that was it. It came from *Macbeth*. Lady Macbeth said it when she and her husband were plotting the old king's murder. And what was the old king's name? Douglas? Donal?

Someone had come out of the bathroom and someone else gone in. Did they always take such ages getting to bed? The lavatory flush roared and a torrent rushed through pipes that seemed to pass under his bed. He heard footsteps across the landing and a door closing. Apparently, they slept in the next room to his. He turned over, longing for the light to go out. It was a pity there was no key in that lock so that he could have locked his door.

As soon as the thought had formed and been uttered in his brain, he thought how fantastic it was. What, lock one's bedroom door in a private house? Suppose his hostess came in in the morning with a cup of tea? She would think it very odd. And she might come in. She had put this bottle in his bed and had placed a glass of water on the table. Of course he couldn't dream of locking the door, and why should he want to? One of them was in the bathroom *again*.

Suddenly he found himself thinking about one of the men he had sacked and who had threatened him. The man had said, "Don't think you'll get away with this, and if you show your ugly face within a mile of my place you may not live to regret it." Of course he had got away with it and had nothing to regret. On the other hand, he hadn't shown himself within a mile of the man's place. . . . The light had gone out at last. Sleep now, he told himself. Empty your mind or think about something nice, your summer holiday in the villa, for instance, think about that.

The gardens would be wonderful with the oleanders and the bougainvillea. And the sun would warm his old bones as he sat on his terrace, looking down through the cleft in the pines at the blue triangle of Mediterranean which was brighter and gentler than that woman's eyes. . . . Never mind the woman, forget her. Perhaps he should have the terrace raised and extended and set up on it that piece of statuary—surely Roman—which he had found in the pinewoods. It would cost a great deal of money, but it was his money. Why shouldn't he spend his own? He must try to be less sensitive, he thought, less troubled by this absurd social conscience which, for some reason, he had lately developed. Not, he reflected with a faint chuckle, that it actually stopped him spending money or enjoying himself. It was a nuisance, that was all.

He would have the terrace extended and maybe a black marble floor laid in the salon. Frasers' profits looked as if they would hit a new high this year. Why not get that fellow Churchouse to do all their printing for them? If he was really down on his luck and desperate he would be bound to work for a cut rate, jump at the chance, no doubt. . . .

God damn it, it was too much! They were talking in there. He could hear their whisperings, rapid, emotional almost, through the wall. They were an absurd couple, no sense of humor between the pair of them. Intense, like characters out of some tragedy.

"The labour we delight in physics pain"—Macbeth had said that, Macbeth who killed the old king. And she had said it to him, Duncan, when he had apologised for the trouble he was causing. The king was called Duncan too. Of course he was.

He was called Duncan and so was the king and he too, in a way, was an old king, the monarch of the Fraser empire. Whisper, whisper, breathed the wall at him.

He sat up and put on the light. With the light on, he felt better. He was sure, though, that he hadn't left those car lights on. "Leave all the rest to me. . . ." Why say that? Why not say what everyone said, "I'll see to everything"? Macbeth and his wife had entertained the old king in their house and murdered him in his bed, although he had done them no harm, done nothing to them but be king. So it wasn't a parallel, was it? For he, Duncan Fraser, had done something, something which might merit vengeance. He had sacked Hugo Crouch and taken away his livelihood. It wasn't a parallel.

He turned off the light, sighed, and lay down again. They were still whispering. He heard the floor creak as one of them came out of the bedroom. It wasn't a parallel—it was much more. Why hadn't he seen that? Lady Macbeth and her husband had had no cause, no cause. . . . A sweat broke out on his face and he reached for the glass of water. But he didn't drink. It was stupid not to but. . . . The morning would soon come. "O, never shall sun that morrow see!" Where did that come from? Need he ask?

Whoever it was in the bathroom had left it and gone back to the other one. But only for a moment. Again he heard the boards creak, again someone was moving about on that dark landing. Dark, yes, pitch dark, for they hadn't switched the light on this time. And Duncan felt then the first thrill of real fear, which didn't subside after the shiver had died but grew and gripped him in a terror the like of which he hadn't known since he was a little boy and had been shut up in the nursery cupboard of his father's manse. He mustn't be afraid, he mustn't. He must think of his heart. Why should they want vengeance? He'd explained. He'd told them the truth, taking the full burden of blame on himself.

The room was so dark that he didn't see the door handle turn. He heard it. It creaked very softly. His heart began a slow, steady pounding and he contracted his body, forcing it back against the wall. Whoever it was had come into the room. He could see the shape of him—or her—as a denser blackness in the dark.

"What . . . ? Who . . . ?" he said, quavering, his throat dry.

The shape grew fluid, glided away, and the door closed softly. They wanted to see if he was asleep. They would kill him when he was asleep. He sat up, switched on the light, and put his face in his hands. "O, never shall sun that morrow see!" He'd put all that furniture against the door, that chest of drawers, his bed, the chair. His throat was parched now and he reached for the water, taking a long draught. It was icy cold.

They weren't whispering any more. They were waiting in silence. He got up and put his coat round him. In the bitter cold he began lugging the furniture away from the walls, lifting the iron bedstead that felt so small and narrow when he was in it but was so hideously weighty.

Straightening up from his second attempt, he felt it, the pain in his chest and down his left arm. It came like a clamp, like a clamp being screwed and at the same time slowly heated red-hot. It took his body in hot iron fingers and squeezed his ribs. And sweat began to pour from him as if the temperature in the room had suddenly risen tremendously. Oh, God, Oh, God, the water in the glass . . . ! They would have to get him a doctor, they would have to, they couldn't be so pitiless. He was old and tired and his heart was bad.

He pulled the coat round the pain and staggered out into the black passage. Their door—where was their door? He found it by fumbling at the walls, scrabbling like an imprisoned animal, and when he found it he kicked it open and swayed on the threshold, holding the pain in both his hands.

They were sitting on their bed with their backs to him, not in bed but sitting there, the shapes of them silhouetted against the light of a small low-bulbed bedlamp.

"Oh, please," he said, "please help me. Don't kill me, I beg you not to kill me. I'll go on my knees to you. I know I've done wrong, I did a terrible thing. I didn't make an error of judgment. I sacked Hugo because he wanted too much for the staff, he wanted more money for everyone and I couldn't let them have it. I wanted my new car and my holidays. I had to have my villa—so beautiful, my villa, my gardens. Ah, God, I know I was greedy but I've borne the guilt of it for months, every day—on my conscience—the guilt of it. . . ." They turned, two white faces, implacable, merciless. They rose and came towards him, scrambling across their bed. "Have pity on me," he screamed. "Don't kill me. I'll give you everything I've got, I'll give you a million . . ."

But they had seized him with their hands and it was too late. She had told him it was too late.

"In our house!" she said.

"Don't," said Hugo. "That's what Lady Macbeth said. What does it matter whether it was in our house or not?"

"I wish I'd never invited him."

"Well, it was your idea. You said let's have him here because he's a widower and lonely. I didn't want him. It was ghastly the way he insisted on talking about firing me when we wanted to keep off the subject at any price. I was utterly fed up when he had to stay the night."

"What do we do now?" said Elizabeth.

"Get the police, I should think, or a doctor. It's stopped raining. I'll get dressed and go."

"But you're not well! You kept throwing up."

"I'm O.K. now. I drank too much brandy. It was such a strain all of it, nobody knowing what to talk about. God, what a business! He was all right when you went into his room just now, wasn't he?"

"Half asleep, I thought. I was going to apologise for all the racket you were making but he seemed nearly asleep. Did you get any of that he was trying to say when he came in here? I didn't."

"No, it was just gibberish. We couldn't have done anything for him, darling. We did try to catch him before he fell."

"I know."

"He had a bad heart."

"In more ways than one, poor old man," said Elizabeth, and she laid a blanket gently over Duncan, though he was past feeling heat or cold or guilt or fear or anything any more.

You Can't Be Too Careful

Della Galway went out with a man for the first (and almost the last) time on her nineteenth birthday. He parked his car, and as they were going into the restaurant she asked him if he had locked all the doors and the boot. When he turned back and said, yes, he'd better do that, she asked him why he didn't have a burglar-proof locking device on the steering wheel.

Her parents had brought her up to be cautious. When she left that happy home in that safe little provincial town, she took her parents' notions with her to London. At first she could only afford the rent of a single room. It upset her that the other tenants often came in late at night and left the front door on the latch. Although her room was at the top of the house and she had nothing worth stealing, she lay in bed sweating with fear. At work it was just the same. Nobody bothered about security measures. Della was always the last to leave, and sometimes she went back two or three times to check that all the office doors and the outer door were shut.

The personnel officer suggested she see a psychiatrist.

Della was very ambitious. She had an economics degree and a business studies diploma, and had come out top at the end of her secretarial course. She knew a psychiatrist would find something wrong with her—they had to earn their money like everyone else—and long sessions of treatment would follow which wouldn't help her towards her goal, that of becoming the company's first woman director. They always held that sort of thing against you.

"That won't be necessary," she said in her brisk way. "It was the firm's property I was worried about. If they like to risk losing their valuable equipment, that's their look-out."

She stopped going back to check the doors—it didn't prey on her mind much as her own safety wasn't involved—and three weeks later two men broke in, stole all the electric typewriters, and damaged the computer beyond repair. It proved her right, but she didn't say so. The threat of the psychiatrist had frightened her so much that she never again aired her burglar obsession at work.

When she got promotion and a salary rise, she decided to get a flat of her own. The landlady was a woman after her own heart. Mrs Swanson liked Della from the first and explained to her, as to a kindred spirit, the security arrangements.

"This is a very nice neighbourhood, Miss Galway, but the crime rate in London is rising all the time, and I always say you can't be too careful."

Della said she couldn't agree more.

"So I always keep this side gate bolted on the inside. The back door into this little yard must also be kept locked and bolted. The bathroom window looks out into the garden, you see, so I like the garden door and the bathroom door to be locked at night too."

"Very wise," said Della, noting that the window in the bed-sitting room had screws fixed to its sashes which prevented its being opened more than six inches. "What did you say the rent was?"

"Twenty pounds a week." Mrs Swanson was a landlady first, and a kindred spirit secondly, so when Della hesitated, she said, "It's a garden flat, completely self-contained and you've got your own phone. I shan't have any trouble in letting it. I've got someone else coming to view it at two."

Della stopped hesitating. She moved in at the end of the week, having supplied Mrs Swanson with references and assured her she was quiet, prudent as to locks and bolts, and not inclined to have "unauthorised" people to stay overnight. By unauthorised people Mrs Swanson meant men. Since the episode over the car on her nineteenth birthday, Della had entered tentatively upon friendships with men, but no man had ever taken her out more than twice and none had ever got as far as to kiss her. She didn't know why this was, as she had always been polite and pleasant, insisting on paying her share, careful to carry her own coat, handbag, and parcels so as to give her escort no trouble, ever watchful of his wallet and keys, offering to have the theatre tickets in her own safe-keep-

ing, and anxious not to keep him out too late. That one after
another men dropped her worried her very little. No spark of
sexual feeling had ever troubled her, and the idea of sharing
her orderly, routine-driven life with a man—untidy, feckless,
casual creatures as they all, with the exception of her father,
seemed to be—was a daunting one. She meant to get to the top
on her own. One day perhaps, when she was about thirty-five
and with a high-powered lady executive's salary, then if some
like-minded, quiet, and prudent man came along. . . . In the
meantime, Mrs Swanson had no need to worry.

Della was very happy with her flat. It was utterly quiet, a
little sanctum tucked at the back of the house. She never heard
a sound from her neighbours in the other parts of the house
and they, of course, never heard a sound from her. She en-
countered them occasionally when crossing from her own front
door to the front door of the house. They were mouselike people who scuttled off to their holes with no more than a nod and
a "good evening." This was as it should be. The flat, too, was
entirely as it should be.

The bed-sitter looked just like a living room by day, for the
bed was let down from a curtained recess in the wall only at
night. Its window overlooked the yard, which Della never
used. She never unbolted the side gate or the back door or,
needless to say, attempted to undo the screws and open the
window more than six inches.

Every evening, when she had washed the dishes and wiped
down every surface in the immaculate, well-fitted kitchen, had
her bath, made her bedtime drink, and let the bed down from
the wall, she went on her security rounds just as her father did
at home. First she unlocked and unbolted the back door and
crossed the yard to check that the side gate was securely fastened. It always was, as no one ever touched it, but Della liked
to make absolutely sure, and sometimes went back several
times in case her eyes had deceived her. Then she bolted and
locked the back door, the garden door, and the bathroom door.
All these doors opened out of a small room, about ten feet
square—Mrs Swanson called it the garden room—which in its

turn could be locked off by yet another door from the kitchen. Della locked it. She rather regretted she couldn't lock the door that led from the kitchen into the bed-sitting room but, owing to some oversight on Mrs Swanson's part, there was no lock on it. However, her own front door in the bed-sitter itself was locked, of course, on the Yale. Finally, before getting into bed, she bolted the front door.

Then she was safe. Though she sometimes got up once or twice more to make assurance trebly sure, she generally settled down at this point into blissful sleep, certain that even the most accomplished of burglars couldn't break in.

There was only one drawback—the rent.

"The flat," said Mrs Swanson, "is really intended for two people. A married couple had it before you, and before that two ladies shared it."

"I couldn't share my bed," said Della with a shudder, "or, come to that, my room."

"If you found a nice friend to share, I wouldn't object to putting up a single bed in the garden room. Then your friend could come and go by the side gate, provided you were prepared to *promise* me it would always be bolted at night."

Della wasn't going to advertise for a flatmate. You couldn't be too careful. Yet she had to find someone if she was going to afford any new winter clothes, not to mention heating the place. It would have to be the right person, someone to fill all her own exacting requirements as well as satisfy Mrs Swanson. . . .

"Ooh, it's lovely!" said Rosamund Vine." It's so quiet and clean. And you've got a garden! You should see the dump I've been living in. It was over-run with mice."

"You don't get mice," said Della repressively, "unless you leave food about."

"I won't do that. I'll be ever so careful. I'll go halves with the rent and I'll have the key to the back door, shall I? That way I won't disturb you if I come in late at night."

"I hope you won't come in late at night," said Della. "Mrs Swanson's very particular about that sort of thing."

"Don't worry." Rosamund sounded rather bitter. "I've nothing and no one to keep me out late. Anyway, the last bus passes the end of the road at a quarter of twelve."

Della pushed aside her misgivings, and Mrs Swanson, interviewing Rosamund, appeared to have none. She made a point of explaining the safety precautions, to which Rosamund listened meekly and with earnest nods of her head. Della was glad this duty hadn't fallen to her, as she didn't want Rosamund to tell exaggerated tales about her at work. So much the better if she could put it all on Mrs Swanson.

Rosamund Vine had been chosen with the care Della devoted to every choice she made. It had taken three weeks of observation and keeping her ears open to select her. It wouldn't do to find someone on too low a salary or, on the other hand, someone with too lofty a position in the company. She didn't like the idea of a spectacularly good-looking girl, for such led hectic lives, or too clever a girl, for such might involve her in tiresome arguments. An elegant girl would fill the cupboards with clothes and the bathroom with cosmetics. A gifted girl would bring in musical instruments or looms or paints or trunks full of books. Only Rosamund, of all the candidates, qualified. She was small and quiet and prettyish, a secretary (though not Della's secretary), the daughter of a clergyman who, by coincidence, had been at the same university at the same time as Della's father. Della, who had much the same attitude as Victorian employers had to their maids' "followers," noted that she had never heard her speak of a boy friend or overheard any cloakroom gossip as to Rosamund's love life.

The two girls settled down happily together. They seldom went out in the evenings. Della always went to bed at eleven sharp and would have relegated Rosamund to her own room at this point but for one small difficulty. With Rosamund in the garden room—necessarily sitting on her bed as there was nowhere else to sit—it wasn't possible for Della to make her security rounds. Only once had she tried doing it with Rosamund looking on.

"Goodness," Rosamund had said, "this place is like Fort Knox. All those keys and bolts! What are you so scared of?"

"Mrs Swanson likes to have the place locked up," said Della, but the next night she made hot drinks for the two of them and sent Rosamund to wait for her in the bed-sitter before creeping out into the yard for a secret check-up.

When she came back Rosamund was examining her bedside table. "Why do you put everything in order like that, Della? Your book at right angles to the table and your cigarette packet at right angles to your book, and, look, your ashtray's exactly an inch from the lamp as if you measured it out."

"Because I'm a naturally tidy person."

"I do think it's funny your smoking. I never would have guessed you smoked till I came to live here. It doesn't sort of seem in character. And your glass of water. Do you want to drink water in the night?"

"Not always," Della said patiently. "But I might want to, and I shouldn't want to have to get up and fetch it, should I?"

Rosamund's questions didn't displease her. It showed that the girl wanted to learn the right way to do things. Della taught her that a room must be dusted every day, the fridge defrosted once a week, the table laid for breakfast before they went to bed, all the windows closed and the catches fastened. She drew Rosamund out as to the places she had previously lived in with a view to contrasting past squalor with present comfort, and she received a shock when Rosamund made it plain that in some of those rooms, attics, converted garages, she had lived with a man. Della made no comment but froze slightly. And Rosamund, thank goodness, seemed to understand her disapproval and didn't go into details. But soon after that she began going out in the evenings.

Della didn't want to know where she was going or with whom. She had plenty to occupy her own evenings, what with the work she brought home, her housework, washing and ironing, her twice-weekly letter to her mother and father, and the commercial Spanish she was teaching herself from gramophone records. It was rather a relief not to have Rosamund fluttering about. Besides, she could do her security rounds in peace. Not, of course, that she could check up on the side gate till Rosamund came in. Necessarily, it had to remain unbolted, and the back door to which Rosamund had the key, unlocked. But always by ten to twelve at the latest she'd hear the side gate open and close and hear Rosamund pause to draw the bolts. Then her feet tiptoeing across the yard, then the back door unlocked, shut, locked. After that, Della could sleep in peace.

The first problem arose when Rosamund came in one night and didn't bolt the gate after her. Della listened carefully in the dark, but she was positive those bolts had not been drawn. Even if the back door was locked, it was unthinkable to leave that side gate on nothing all night but its flimsy latch. She put on her dressing gown and went through the kitchen into the garden room. Rosamund was already in bed, her clothes flung about on the coverlet. Della picked them up and folded them. She was coming back from the yard, having fastened those bolts, when Rosamund sat up and said, "What's the matter? Can't you sleep?"

"Mrs Swanson," said Della with a light indulgent laugh, "wouldn't be able to sleep if she knew you'd left that side gate unbolted."

"Did I? Honestly, Della, I don't know what I'm doing half the time. I can't think of anyone but Chris. He's the most marvellous person and I do think he's just as mad about me as I am about him. I feel as if he's changed my whole life."

Della let her spend nearly all the following evening describing the marvellous Chris, how brilliant he was—though at present unable to get a job fitting his talents—how amusing, how highly educated—though so poor as to be reduced to borrowing a friend's room while that friend was away. She listened and smiled and made appropriate remarks, but she wondered when she had last been so bored. Every time she got up to try and play one of her Spanish records, Rosamund was off again on another facet of Chris's dazzling personality, until at last

Della had to say she had a headache and would Rosamund mind leaving her on her own for a bit?

"Anyway, you'll see him tomorrow. I've asked him for a meal."

Unluckily, this happened to be the evening Della was going to supper with her aunt on the other side of London. They had evidently enjoyed themselves, judging by the mess in the kitchen, Della thought when she got home. There were few things she disliked more than wet dishes left to drain. Rosamund was asleep. Della crept out into the yard and checked that the bolts were fastened.

"I heard you wandering about ever so late," said Rosamund in the morning. "Were you upset about anything?"

"Certainly not. I simply found it rather hard to get to sleep because it was past my normal time."

"Aren't you funny?" said Rosamund, and she giggled.

The next night she missed the last bus.

Della had passed a pleasant evening, studying firstly the firm's annual report, then doing a Spanish exercise. By eleven she was in bed, reading the memoirs of a woman company chairman. Her bedside light went off at half-past and she lay in the dark waiting for the sound of the side gate.

Her clock had luminous hands, and when they passed ten to twelve she began to feel a nasty, tingly, jumping sensation all over her body. She put on the light, switched it off immediately. She didn't want Rosamund bursting in with all her silly questions and comments. But Rosamund didn't burst in, and the hands of the clock closed together on midnight. There was no doubt about it. The last bus had gone and Rosamund hadn't been on it.

Well, the silly girl needn't think she was going to stand this sort of thing. She'd bolt that side gate herself and Rosamund could stay out in the street all night. Of course she might ring the front-door bell, she was silly and inconsiderate enough to do that, but it couldn't be helped. Della would far rather be awakened at one or two o'clock than lie there knowing that side gate was open for anyone to come in. She put on her dressing gown and made her way through the spotless kitchen to the garden room. Rosamund had hung a silly sort of curtain over the back door, not a curtain really but a rather dirty Indian bedspread. Della lifted it distastefully—and then she realised. She couldn't bolt the side gate because the back door into the yard was locked and Rosamund had the key.

A practical person like herself wasn't going to be done that way. She'd go out by the front door, walk round to the side entrance and—but, no, that wouldn't work either. If she opened the gate and bolted it on the inside, she'd simply find herself bolted inside the yard. The only thing was to climb out of the window. She tried desperately to undo the window screws, but they had seized up from years of disuse and she couldn't shift them. Trembling now, she sat down on the edge of her bed and lit a cigarette. For the first time in her life she was in an insecure place by night, alone in a London flat, with nothing to separate her from hordes of rapacious burglars but a feeble back-door lock which any tyro of a thief could pick open in five minutes.

How criminally careless of Mrs Swanson not to have provided the door between the bed-sitter and the kitchen with a lock! There was no heavy piece of furniture she could place against the door. The phone was by her bed, of course. But if she heard a sound and dialled for the police, was there a chance of their getting there before she was murdered and the place ransacked?

What Mrs Swanson *had* provided was one of the most fearsome-looking breadknives Della had ever seen. She fetched it from the kitchen and put it under her pillow. Its presence made her feel slightly safer, but suppose she didn't wake up when the man came in, suppose . . . ? That was ridiculous, she wouldn't sleep at all. Exhausted, shaken, feeling physically sick, she crawled under the bedclothes and, after concentrated thought, put the light out. Perhaps, if there was no light on, he would go past her, not know she was there, make his way into the main part of the house, and if by then she hadn't actually died of fright . . .

At twenty minutes past one, when she had reached the point of deciding to phone for a car to take her to an hotel, the side gate clicked and Rosamund entered the yard. Della fell back against the pillows with a relief so tremendous that she couldn't even bother to go out and check the bolts. So what if it wasn't bolted? The man would have to pass Rosamund first, kill her first. Della found she didn't care at all about what might happen to Rosamund, only about her own safety.

She sneaked out at half past six to put the knife back, and she was sullenly eating her breakfast, the flat immaculate, when Rosamund appeared at eight.

"I missed the last bus. I had to get a taxi."

"You could have phoned."

"Goodness, you sound just like my mother. It was bad enough having to get up and . . ." Rosamund blushed and put her hand over her mouth. "I mean, go *out* and get that taxi and. . . . Well, I wasn't all that late," she muttered.

Her little slip of the tongue hadn't been lost on Della. But she was too tired to make any rejoinder beyond saying that Mrs Swanson would be very annoyed if she knew, and would Rosamund give her fair warning next time she intended to be late? Rosamund said when they met again that evening that she couldn't give her fair warning as she could never be sure herself. Della said no more. What, anyway, would be the use of knowing what time Rosamund was coming in when she couldn't bolt the gate?

Three mornings later her temper flared.

On two of the intervening nights Rosamund had missed the last bus. The funny thing was that she didn't look at all tired or jaded, while Della was worn out. For three hours on the previous night she had lain stiffly clutching the breadknife while the old house creaked about her and the side gate rattled in the wind.

"I don't know why you bother to come home at all."

"Won't you mind if I don't?"

"Not a bit. Do as you like."

Stealthily, before Rosamund left the flat by the front door,

Della slipped out and bolted the gate. Rosamund, of course (being utterly imprudent), didn't check the gate before she locked the back door. Della fell into a heavy sleep at ten o'clock, to be awakened just after two by a thudding on the side gate followed by a frenzied ringing of the front-door bell.

"You locked me out!" Rosamund sobbed. "Even my mother never did that. I was locked out in the street and I'm frozen. What have I done to you that you treat me like that?"

"You said you weren't coming home."

"I wasn't going to, but we went out and Chris forgot his key. He's had to sleep at a friend's place. I wish I'd gone there too!"

They were evidently two of a kind. Well-suited, Della thought. Although it was nearly half past two in the morning, this seemed the best moment to have things out. She addressed Rosamund in her precise, schoolmistressy voice.

"I think we'll have to make other arrangements, Rosamund. Your ways aren't my ways, and we don't really get on, do we? You can stay here till you find somewhere else, but I'd like to start looking round straightaway."

"But what have I *done?* I haven't made a noise or had my friends here. I haven't even used your phone, not once. Honestly, Della, I've done my best to keep the place clean and tidy, and it's nearly killed me!"

"I've explained what I mean. We're not the same kind of people."

"I'll go on Saturday. I'll go to my mother—it won't be any worse, God knows—and then maybe Chris and I . . ."

"You'd better go to bed now," Della said coldly, but she couldn't get any sleep herself. She was wondering how she had been such a bad judge of character, and wondering too what she was going to do about the rent. Find someone else, of course. An older woman perhaps, a widow or a middle-aged spinster. . . .

What she was determined not to do was reveal to Rosamund, at this late stage, her anxiety about the side gate. If anything remained to comfort her, it was the knowledge that Rosamund thought her strong, mature, and sensible. But not revealing it brought her an almost unbearable agony. For Rosamund seemed to think the very sight of her would be an embarrassment to Della. Each evening she was gone from the flat before Della got home, and each time she had gone out leaving the side gate unbolted and the back door locked. Della had no way of knowing whether she would come in on the last bus or get a taxi or be seen home in the small hours by Chris. She didn't know whether Chris lived near or far away, and now she wished she had listened more closely to Rosamund's confidences and asked a few questions of her own. Instead, she had only thought with a shudder how nasty it must be to have to sleep with a man, and had wondered if she would ever bring herself to face the prospect.

Each night she took the breadknife to bed with her, confirmed in her conviction that she wasn't being unreasonable when one of the mouselike people whom she met in the hall told her the house next door had been broken into and its old woman occupant knocked on the head. Rosamund came in once at one, once at half past two, and once she didn't come in at all. Della got great bags under her eyes and her skin looked grey. She fell asleep over her desk at work, while a bright-eyed, vivacious Rosamund regaled her friends in the cloak-room about the joys of her relationship with Chris.

But now there was only one more night to go. . . .

Rosamund had left a note to say she wouldn't be home. She'd see Della on the following evening when she collected her cases to take them to her mother. But she'd left the side gate unbolted. Della seriously considered bolting it and then climbing back over it into the side entrance, but it was too high and smooth for her to climb and there wasn't a ladder. Nothing for it but to begin her vigil with the cigarettes, the glass of water, the phone, and the breadknife. It ought to have been easier, this last night, just because it was the last. Instead, it was worse than any of the others. She lay in the dark, thinking of the old woman next door, of the house that was precisely the same as the one next door, and of the intruder who now knew the best and simplest way in. She tried to think of something else, anything else, but the strongest instinct of all over-rode all her feeble attempts to concentrate on tomorrow, on work, on ambition, on the freedom and peace of tomorrow when that gate would be fastened for good, never again to be opened.

Rosamund had said she wouldn't be in. But you couldn't rely on a word she said. Della wasn't, therefore, surprised (though she was overwhelmingly relieved) to hear the gate click just before two. Sighing with a kind of ecstasy—for to-morrow had come—she listened for the sound of the bolts being drawn across. The sound didn't come. Well, that was a small thing. She'd fasten the bolts herself when Rosamund was in bed. She heard footsteps moving very softly, and then the back door was unlocked. Rosamund took a longer time than usual about unlocking it, but maybe she was tired or drunk or heaven knew what.

Silence.

Then the back door creaked and made rattling sounds as if Rosamund hadn't bothered to relock it. Wearily, Della hoisted herself out of bed and slipped her dressing gown round her. As she did so, the kitchen light came on. The light showed round the edges of the old door in a brilliant phosphorescent rectangle. That wasn't like Rosamund, who never went into the kitchen, who fell immediately into bed without even bothering to wash her face. A long shiver ran through Della. Her body taut but trembling, she listened. Footsteps were crossing the kitchen floor and the fridge door was opened. She heard the sounds of fumbling in cupboards, a drawer was opened, and silver rattled. She wanted to call out, "Rosamund, Rosamund, is that you?" but she had no voice. Her mouth was dry and her voice had gone. Something occurred to her that had never struck her before. It struck her with a great thrust of terror. How would she know, how had she ever known, whether it was Rosamund or another who entered the flat by the side gate and the frail back door?

Then there came a cough.

It was a slight cough, the sound of someone clearing his

throat, but it was unmistakably *his* throat. There was a man in the kitchen.

Della forgot the phone. She remembered—though she had scarcely for a moment forgotten her—the old woman next door. Blind terror thrust her to her feet, plunged her hand under the pillow for the knife. She opened the kitchen door, and he was there, a tall man, young and strong, standing right there on the threshold with Mrs Swanson's silver in one hand and Mrs Swanson's heavy iron pan in the other. Della didn't hesitate. She struck hard with the knife, struck again and again until the bright blood flew across the white walls and the clean ironing and the table neatly laid for breakfast.

The policeman was very nice to Rosamund Vine. He called her by her christian name and gave her a cup of coffee. She drank the coffee, though she didn't really want it as she had had a cup at the hospital when they told her Chris was dead.

"Tell me about last night, will you, Rosamund?"

"I'd been out with my boy friend—Chris—Chris Maitland. He'd forgotten his key and he hadn't anywhere to sleep, so I said to come back with me. He was going to leave early in the morning before she—before Della was up. We were going to be very careful about that. And we were terribly quiet. We crept in at about two."

"You didn't call out?"

"No, we thought she was asleep. That's why we didn't speak to each other, not even in whispers. But she must have heard us." Her voice broke a little. "I went straight to bed. Chris was hungry. I said if he was as quiet as a mouse he could get himself something from the fridge, and I told him where the knives and forks and plates were. The next thing I heard this ghastly scream and I ran out and—and Chris was. . . . There was blood everywhere. . . ."

The policeman waited until she was calmer.

"Why do you think she attacked him with a knife?" he asked.

"I don't know."

"I think you do, Rosamund."

"Perhaps I do." Rosamund looked down. "She didn't like me going out."

"Because she was afraid of being there alone?"

"Della Galway," said Rosamund, "wasn't afraid of anything. Mrs Swanson was nervous about burglars, but Della wasn't. Everyone in the house knew about the woman next door getting coshed, and they were all nervous. Except Della. She didn't even mention it to me, and she must have known."

"So she didn't think Chris was a burglar?"

"Of course she didn't." Rosamund started to cry. "She saw a man—my man. She couldn't get one of her own. Every time I tried to talk about him she went all cold and standoffish. She heard us come in last night and she understood and—and it sent her over the edge. It drove her crazy. I'd heard they wanted her to see a psychiatrist at work, and now I know why."

The policeman shivered a little, in spite of his long experience. Fear of burglars he could understand, but this. . . . "She'll see one now," he said, and then he sent the weeping girl home to her mother.

The Double

Strange dishevelled women who had the air of witches sat round the table in Mrs Cleasant's drawing room. One of them, a notable medium, seemed to be making some sort of divination with a pack of Tarot cards. Later on, when it got dark, they would go on to table-turning. The aim was to raise up the spirit of Mr Cleasant, one year dead, and also perhaps, Peter thought with anger and disgust, to frighten Lisa out of her wits.

"Where are you going?" said Mrs Cleasant when Lisa came back with her coat on.

Peter answered for her. "I'm taking her for a walk in Holland Park, and then we'll have a meal somewhere."

"Holland Park?" said the medium. If a corpse could have spoken it would have had a voice like hers. "Take care, be watchful. That place has a reputation."

The witch women looked at her expectantly, but the medium had returned to her Tarot and was eyeing the Empress, which she had brought within an inch or two of her long nose. Peter was sickened by the lot of them. Six months to go, he thought, and he'd take her out of this—this coven.

It was a Sunday afternoon in spring, and the air in the park was fresh and clean, almost like country air. Peter drew in great gulps of it, cleansing himself of the atmosphere of that drawing room. He wished Lisa would unwind, be less nervous and strung-up. The hand he wasn't holding kept going up to the charm she wore on a chain round her neck or straying out to knock on wood as they passed a fence.

Suddenly she said, "What did that woman mean about the park's reputation?"

"Some occult rubbish. How should I know? I hate that sort of thing."

"So do I," she said, "but I'm afraid of it."

"When we're married you'll never have to have any more to

do with it. I'll see to that. God, I wish we could get married now or you'd come and live with me till we can."

"I can't marry you till I'm eighteen without Mummy's permission, and if I go and live with you they'll make me a ward of court."

"Surely not, Lisa."

"Anyway, there's only six months to wait. It's hard for me too. Don't you think I'd rather live with you than with Mummy?"

The childish rejoinder made him smile. "Come on, try and look a bit more cheerful. I want to take your photograph. If I can't have you, I'll have your picture." They had reached a sunny open space where he sat her on a log and told her to smile. He got the camera out of its case. "Don't look at those people, darling. Look at me."

It was a pity the man and the girl had chosen that moment to sit down on the wooden seat.

"Lisa!" he said sharply, and then he wished he hadn't, for her face crumpled with distress. He went up to her. "What's the matter now, Lisa?"

"Look at that girl," she said.

"All right. What about her?"

"She's exactly like me. She's my double."

"Nonsense. What makes you say that? Her hair's the same colour and you're about the same build, but apart from that, there's no resemblance. She's years older than you and she's . . ."

"Peter, you must see it! She might be my twin. Look, the man with her has noticed. He looked at me and said something to her and then they both looked."

He couldn't see more than a superficial similarity. "Well, supposing she were your double, which I don't for a moment admit, so what? Why get in such a state about it?"

"Don't you know about doubles? Don't you know that if you see your double, you're seeing your own death, you die within the year?"

"Oh, Lisa, come *on*. I never heard anything so stupid. This is more rubbish you've picked up from those crazy old witches. It's just sick superstition." But nothing he could say calmed her. Her face had grown white and her eyes troubled. Worried for her rather than angry, he put out his hand and helped her to her feet. She leant against him, trembling, and he saw she was clutching her amulet. "Let's go," he said. "We'll find another place to take your picture. Don't look at her if it upsets you. Forget her."

When they had gone off along the path, the man on the seat said to his companion, "Couldn't you really see that girl was the image of you?"

"I've already told you, no."

"Of course you look a good deal older and harder, I'll give you that."

"Thank you."

"But you're almost her double. Take away a dozen years and a dozen love affairs, and you'd *be* her double."

"Stephen, if you're trying to start another row, just say so and I'll go home."

"I'm not starting anything. I'm fascinated by an extraordinary phenomenon. Holland Park's known to be a strange place. There's a legend you can see your own double there."

"I never heard that."

"Nevertheless, my dear Zoe, it is so.

"'The Magus, Zoroaster, my dear child,
   Saw his own image walking in the garden.'"

"Who said that?"

"Shelley. Superstition has it that if you see your own image you die within the year."

She turned slowly to look at him. "Do you want me to die within the year, Stephen?"

He laughed. "Oh, you won't die. You didn't see her, she saw you. And it frightened her. He was taking her photograph, did you see? I wish I'd asked him to take one of you two together. Why don't we see if we can catch them up?"

"You know, you have a sick imagination."

"No, only a healthy curiosity. Come along now, if we walk fast we'll catch them up by the gate."

"If it amuses you," said Zoe.

Peter and Lisa didn't see the other couple approaching. They were walking with their arms round each other, and Peter had managed to distract her from the subject of her double by talking of their wedding plans. At the northern gate someone behind him called out, "Excuse me!" and he turned to see the man who had been sitting on the seat.

"Yes?" he said rather stiffly.

"I expect you'll think this is frightful cheek, but I saw you back there and I was absolutely—well, struck by the likeness between my girl friend and the young lady with you. There is a terrific likeness, isn't there?"

"I don't see it," said Peter, not daring to look at Lisa. What a beastly thing to happen! He felt dismay. "Frankly, I don't see any resemblance at all."

"Oh, but you must. Look, what I want is for you to do me an enormous favour and take a picture of them together. Will you? Do say you will."

Peter was about to refuse, and not politely, when Lisa said, "Why not? Of course he will. It's such a funny coincidence, we ought to have a record of it."

"Good girl! We'd better introduce ourselves then, hadn't we? I'm Stephen Davidson and this is Zoe Conti."

"Lisa Cleasant and Peter Milton," said Peter, still half stunned by Lisa's warm response.

"Hallo, Lisa and Peter. Lovely to know you. Now you two girls go and stand over there in that spot of sunshine. . . ."

So Peter took the photograph and said he'd send Stephen and Zoe a copy when the film was developed. She gave him the address of the flat she and Stephen shared and he noted it was in the next street but one to his. They might have walked there together, which was what Stephen, remarking on this second coincidence, seemed to want. But seeing the tense, strained look in Lisa's eyes, Peter refused, and they separated in Holland Park Avenue.

"You didn't mind about not going with them, did you?" said Lisa.

"Of course not. I'd rather be alone with you."

"I'm glad," she said, and then, "I did it for you."

He understood. She had done it for him, to prove to him she could conquer those superstitious terrors. For his sake, because he wanted it, she would try. He took her in his arms and kissed her.

She leant against him. He could feel her heart beating. "I shan't tell anyone else about it," she said, and he knew she meant her mother and the witch women.

When the film was developed he didn't show it to her. Zoe and Stephen should have their copy and that would be an end of the whole incident. But when he was putting it into an envelope, he realised he would have to write a covering note, which was a bore as he didn't like writing letters. Besides, if he was going to take it to the post, he might as well take it to their home. This, one evening, he did.

He had no intention of going in. But as he was slipping the envelope into the letter box, Zoe appeared behind him on the steps.

"Come in and have a drink."

He couldn't think of an excuse, so he accepted. She led him up two flights of stairs, looking at the photograph as she went.

"So much for this fantastic likeness," she said. "Could you ever see it?"

Peter said he couldn't, wondering how Lisa could have been so silly as to fancy she had seen her double in this woman of thirty, who tonight had a drawn and haggard look. "It was mostly in your friend's imagination," he said as they entered the flat. "We'll see what he says about it now."

For a moment she didn't answer. When her reply came, it was brusque. "He's left me."

Peter was embarrassed. "I'm sorry." He looked into her face, at the eyes whose dark sockets were like bruises. "Are you very unhappy?"

"I shan't take an overdose, if that's what you mean. We'd

been together for four years. It's hard to take. But I won't bore you with it. Let's talk about something else."

Peter had only meant to stay half an hour, but the half-hour grew into an hour, and when Zoe said she was going to cook her dinner and would he stay and have it with her, he agreed. She was interesting to talk to. She was a music therapist, and she talked about her work and played records. When they had finished their meal, a simple but excellent one, she reverted to her own private life and told him something of her long and fraught relationship with Stephen. But she spoke without self-pity. And she could listen as well as talk. It meant something to him to be able to confide in a mature, well-balanced woman who heard him out without interruption while he spoke of himself and Lisa, how they were going to be married when she was eighteen and when she would inherit half her dead father's fortune. Not, he said, that the money had anything to do with it. He'd have preferred her to be penniless. All he wanted was to get her away from that unhealthy atmosphere of dabbling with the occult, from that cloistral home where she was sheltered yet corrupted.

"What is she afraid of?" asked Zoe when he told her about the wood-touching and the indispensable amulet.

He shrugged. "Of fate? Of some avenging fury that resents her happiness?"

"Or of loss," said Zoe. "She lost her father. Perhaps she's afraid of losing you."

"That's the last thing she need be afraid of," he said.

It was midnight before he left. The next day he meant to tell Lisa where he had been. There were no secrets between them. But Lisa was nervous and uneasy—she and Mrs Cleasant had been to a spiritualist meeting—and he thought it unwise to raise once more a subject that was better forgotten. So he said nothing. After all, he would never see Zoe again.

But a month or so later, a month in which he and Lisa had been happy and tranquil together, he met the older girl by chance in the Portobello Road. While they talked, it occurred to him that he had eaten a meal in her flat and that he owed her dinner. He and Lisa would take her out to dinner. In her present mood, Lisa would like that, and it would be good for her to see, after the lapse of time, how her superstitiousness had led her into error. He put the invitation to Zoe who hesitated, then accepted when he explained it would be a threesome. Dinner, then, in a fortnight's time, and he and Lisa would call for her.

"I met that girl Zoe and asked her to have dinner with us. All right with you?"

The frightened-child look came back into Lisa's face.

"Oh, no, Peter! I thought you understood, I don't ever want to see her again."

"But why not? You've seen how silly those ideas of yours were. And Stephen won't be there. I know you didn't like him and neither did I. But they're not together any more. He's left her."

She shivered. "Let's not get to know her, Peter."

"I've invited her," he said. "I can't go back on that now."

When the evening came, Zoe appeared at her door in a long gown, her hair dressed on top of her head. She looked majestic, mysteriously changed.

"Where's Lisa?" she asked.

"She couldn't come. She and her mother are going on holiday to Greece at the end of the week and she's busy packing." Part of this was true. He said it confidently, as if it were wholly true. He couldn't take his eyes off the new, transformed Zoe, and he was glad he had booked a table in an exclusive restaurant.

In the soft lamplight her youth had come back to her. And for the first time he was aware of the likeness between her and Lisa. The older and the younger sister, by a trickery of light and cosmetics and maybe of his own wistful imagination, had met in years and become twins. It might have been his Lisa who spoke to him across the table, across the silver and glass and the single rose in a vase, but a Lisa whom life and experience had matured. Never could Lisa have talked like this of books and music and travel, or listened to him so responsively or advised with such wisdom. He was sorry when the evening came to an end and he left her at her door.

Lisa seemed to have forgotten his engagement to dine with Zoe. She didn't mention it, so he didn't either. On the following morning she was to leave with her mother for the month's holiday the doctor had recommended for Mrs Cleasant's health.

"I wish I wasn't going," she said to Peter. "You don't know how I'll miss you."

"Shan't I miss you?"

"Take care of yourself, I'll worry in case anything happens to you. You mustn't laugh, but when my father was alive and went away from us, I used to listen to the news four or five times a day in case there was a plane crash or a disaster."

"You're the one that's going away, Lisa."

"It comes to the same thing." She put up her hand and the charm she wore. "I've got this, but you . . . Would you take my four-leaved clover if I gave it to you?"

"I thought you'd given up all that nonsense," he said, and his disappointment in her soured their farewells. She kissed him good-bye with a kind of passionate sadness.

"Write to me," she said. "I'll write every day."

Her letters started coming at the end of the first week. They were the first he had ever had from her and they were like school essays written by a geography student, with love messages for the class teacher inserted here and there. They left him unsatisfied, a little peevish. He was lonely without her, but frightened of the image of her he carried with him. He needed someone with whom to talk it over and, after a few days of indecision, he telephoned Zoe. Ten minutes later he was in her flat, drinking her coffee and listening to her music. To be with her was a greater comfort than he had thought possible, for in the turn of her head, a certain way of hers of smiling, he caught glimpses of Lisa.

And yet on that occasion he said nothing of his fears but "I can't understand why I thought you and Lisa weren't alike."

"I didn't see it."

"It's almost overpowering, it's uncanny."

She smiled. "If it helps you to come and see me to get through the time while she's away, that's all right with me, Peter. I can understand that I remind you of her and that makes things easier for you."

"It isn't only that," he said. "You mustn't think it's only that."

She said no more. It wasn't her way to probe, to hold inquisitions, or to set an egotistical value on herself. But the next time they were together, he explained without being asked, and his explanation was appalling to him, the words more powerful and revealing than the thoughts from which they had sprung.

"It isn't true you remind me of Lisa. That's not it. It's that I see in you what she might become, only she never will."

"Who would want to be like me?"

"Everyone. Every young girl. Because you're what a woman should be, Zoe, clever and sane and kind and self-reliant and—beautiful."

"And if that's true," she said lightly, "though I disagree, why shouldn't Lisa become like that?"

"Because when she's eighteen she'll be rich, an heiress. She'll never have to work for her living or struggle or learn. We'll live in a house near her mother and she'll get like her mother, vain and neurotic, living on sleeping pills, spending all her time with spiritualists and getting involved in sick cults. When I look at you I don't see Lisa's double. I see her, an alternative she, if you like, thirteen years ahead in time if another path had been marked out for her in life. And at the same time I see you as you'd be if you'd led the sort of life she must and will lead."

"You can help her not to lead that life if you love her," said Zoe.

And then Lisa's letters stopped coming. A week went by without a letter. He had resolved, because of what was happening to him, not to see Zoe again. But she lived so near and he thought of her so often that he was unable to resist. He went to her and told a lie that he convinced himself might be the truth. Lisa was too young to have a firm and faithful love for anyone. Her letters had grown cold and had finally ceased to come. Zoe listened to him, to his urgent persuasions, his comparison of his forsaken state with her own, and when he kissed her, she responded at first with doubts, then with an ardour born of her own loneliness. They made love. When, later, he asked her if he might stay the night, she said he could and he did.

After that, he spent every night with her. He hardly went home. When he did he found ten letters waiting for him on the doormat. Lisa and her mother had gone on to some Aegean island—the home of a mystic Mrs Cleasant longed to meet—where the posts were hazardous. He read the childish letters, the "darling Peter, I miss you, I'll never go away again" with impatience and with guilt, and then he went back to Zoe.

Why did he have to mention those letters to her? He wished he hadn't. It was for her wisdom and her honesty that he had wanted her, and now those very qualities were striking back at him.

"When is she coming home?"

"Next Saturday," he said.

"Peter, I don't know what you mean to do, leave me and marry her, or leave her and stay with me. But you must tell her about us, whatever you decide."

"I can't do that!"

"You must. Either way, you must. And if you mean to stay with me, what alternative have you?"

Stay with them both until he was sure, until he knew for certain. "You know I can't be without you, Zoe. But I can't tell her, not yet. She's such a child."

"You're going to marry that child. You love her."

"Do I?" he said. "I thought I did."

"I won't be a party to deceiving her, Peter. You must understand that. If you won't promise to tell her, I can't see you again."

Perhaps when he saw Lisa. . . . He went across the park to her mother's house on the Sunday evening. The medium was there and another woman who looked like a participant in a Black Mass, earnestly listening to Mrs Cleasant's account of the mystic and his investigations into the mysteries of the Great Pyramid. Lisa rushed into his arms, actually crying with happiness.

"This child has dreamed about you every night, Peter," said Mrs Cleasant with one of her weird, faraway looks. "Such dreams she has had! Of course she's psychic like me." When we knew the posts were delayed I wanted her to get a message through to you by the Power of Thought, but she was unwilling."

"I knew you wouldn't like it," said Lisa. She sat on his knee, in his arms. Of course he couldn't tell her. In time, maybe, if he got their wedding postponed and cooled things and . . . But it was out of the question to tell her now.

He told Zoe he had. In order to see her again, he had to do that.

"How did she take it?"

"Oh, quite well," he lied. "A lot of men have been paying her attention on holiday. I think she's just beginning to realise I'm not the only man in the world."

"And she accepts—us?"

Why did she have to persist, why make it so painful for him? He spoke boldly but with an inner self-disgust.

"I daresay she sees it as a let-out for her own freedom."

She was convinced. The habitual truth-teller is reluctant to detect falsehood in others. "Of course I've only met her once, and then only for a few minutes. But I wonder if you weren't deceiving yourself, Peter, when you said she loved you so much. You aren't going to see her again?"

He said he wasn't. He said it was all over, they had parted. But the enormity of what he had done appalled him. And when next he was with Lisa he found himself telling her all over again, and meaning it, how much he loved her and longed to take her away. Was he going to sacrifice that childish passionate love for a woman five years older than himself? They were, in many ways, so alike. Suppose, in time to come, he grew tired of the one and regretted the other? Yet, that night, he went back to Zoe.

With a skilful but frightening intrigue, he divided his time between the one and the other. It wasn't too difficult. Social—and occult—demands were always being made on Lisa. Zoe believed him when he said he had been kept late at work. Autumn came, and it was still going on, this double life. His need for, his dependence on, Zoe intensified and he had begun to resent every moment he spent away from her. But Lisa and her mother had fixed his wedding date and with fatality he accepted its inexorable approach.

On an afternoon in October he was to meet Zoe in Holland Park, by the northern gate. Lisa was going for a fitting of her wedding dress and afterwards to dine with her mother in what he called the medium's lair. So that was all right. He waited by the gate for nearly an hour. When Zoe didn't come, he went to her flat but received no answer to his ring. From his own home he telephoned her five times during the evening, but each time the bell rang into emptiness. He passed a sleepless night, the first night he had been on his own for four months.

All the next day, from work, he kept trying to call her, and for the first time since he had known her he made no call to Lisa. But his own phone was ringing when he got home at six. Of course it was Zoe, it must be. He took up the receiver and heard the fraught voice of Mrs Cleasant.

"Peter?"

Disappointment hurt him like pain. "Yes," he said. "How are you? How's Lisa?"

"Peter, I have very bad news. I think you had better come here. Yes, now. At once."

"What is it? Has anything happened to Lisa?"

"Lisa has—has passed over. Last night she took an overdose of my pills. I found her dead this morning."

He went out again at once. In the park, at dusk, the leaves were dying and livid, some already fallen. At this point, when they had been showing their first green of spring, he had taken the photograph; at this, he had seated her in a sunny open space and she had seen Zoe.

Mrs Cleasant wasn't alone. Some of the members of her magic circle were with her, but she was calmer than he had ever seen her and he guessed she was drugged.

"How did it happen?" he said.

"I told you. She took an overdose."

"But—why?" He shrank away from the medium's eyes, which, staring, seemed to see ghosts behind him.

"Nothing to do with you, Peter," said Mrs Cleasant. "She loved you, you know that. And she was so happy yesterday. Her fitting was cancelled. She said she wanted fresh air because it was such a lovely day, and then she'd walk over to you. She'd thrown away her charm—that amulet she wore—because she said you didn't like it. I told her not to, as it was a harmless thing and might do good. Who knows? If she had been wearing it . . ."

"Ah, if she had been under the Protection!" said the medium.

Mrs Cleasant went on, "We were going out to dinner. I waited and waited for her. When she didn't come I went alone. I thought she was with you, safe with you. But I came back early and there she was, looking so tired and afraid. She said she was going to bed. I asked her if there was anything wrong and she said . . ." But Mrs Cleasant's voice quavered into sobs and the witch women fluttered about her, touching her and murmuring.

It was the medium who explained in her corpse voice. "She said she had seen her own double in the park."

"But that was six months ago," he burst out. "That was in April!"

"No, she saw her own double yesterday afternoon, her image walking in the garden. And she dared to speak to it. Who can tell what your own death will tell you when you dare to address it?"

He ran away from them then, out of the house. He hailed a taxi and in a shaking whisper asked the driver to take him to where Zoe lived. All the lights were on in her windows. He rang the bell, rang it again and again. Then, while the lights still blazed but she didn't come down, he hammered on the door with his fists, calling her name. When he knew she wasn't going to come, that he had lost her and her image, her double and her, for ever, he sank down on the doorstep and wept.

The taxi driver, returning along the street in search of a fare, supposed him to be drunk, and learning his address from the broken mutterings, took him home.

Venus' Fly-trap

As soon as Daphne had taken off her hat and put it on Merle's bed, Merle picked it up and rammed it on her own yellow curls. It was a red felt hat and by chance it matched Merle's red dress.

"It's a funny thing, dear," said Merle, looking at herself in the dressing-table mirror, "but anyone seeing us two—any outsider, I mean—would never think that I was the single one and you'd had all those husbands and children."

"I only had two husbands and three children," said Daphne.

"You know what I mean," said Merle, and Daphne, standing beside her friend, had to admit that she did. Merle was so big, so pink and overflowing and female, while she—well, she had given up pretending she was anything but a little dried-up widow, seventy years old and looking every day of it.

Merle took off the hat and placed it beside the doll whose yellow satin skirts concealed her nightdress and her bag of hair rollers. "I'll show you the flat and then we'll have a sherry and put our feet up. I got some of that walnut brown in. You see I haven't forgotten your tastes even after forty years."

Daphne didn't say it was dry sherry she had then, and still, preferred. She trotted meekly after Merle. She was just beginning to be aware of the intense heat. Clouds of warmth seemed to breathe out of the embossed wallpaper and up through the lush, furry carpets.

"I really am thrilled about you coming to live in this block, dear. This is my little spare room. I like to think I can put up a friend if I want. Not that many of them come. Between you and me, dear, people rather resent my having done so well for myself and all on my own initiative. People are so mean-spirited, I've noticed that as I've got older. That's why I was so thrilled when you agreed to come here. I mean, when *someone* took my advice."

"You've made it all very nice," said Daphne.

"Well, I always say the flat had the potential and I had the taste. Of course, yours is much smaller and, frankly, I wouldn't say it lends itself to a very ambitious décor. In your place, the first thing I'd do is have central heating put in."

"I expect I will if I can afford it."

"You know, Daphne, there are some things we owe it to ourselves to afford. But you know your own business best and I wouldn't dream of interfering. If the cold gets you down you're welcome up here at any time. *Any* time, I mean that. Now this is my drawing room, my *pièce de résistance*."

Merle opened the door with the air of a girl lifting the lid of a jewel case that holds a lover's gift.

"What a lot of plants," said Daphne faintly.

"I was always mad about plants. My first business venture was a florist's. I could have made a little goldmine out of that if my partner hadn't been so wickedly vindictive. She was determined to oust me from the first. D'you like my suite? I had it completely redone in oyster satin last year and I do think it's a success."

The atmosphere was that of a hothouse. The chairs, the sofa, the lamps, the little piecrust tables with their load of bibelots were islanded in the centre of the large room. No, not an island perhaps, Daphne thought, but a clearing in a tropical jungle. Shelves, window sills, white troughs on white wrought-iron legs burgeoned with lush trailing growth, green, glossy, frondy, all quite immobile and all giving forth a strange green scent.

"They take up all my time. It's not just the watering and watching the temperature and so on. Plants know when you love them. They only flourish in an atmosphere of love. I honestly don't believe you'd find a better specimen of an opuntia in London than mine. I'm particularly proud of the peperomias and the zygocacti too. Of course, I expect you've seen them growing in their natural habitat with all your mad rushing around those foreign places."

"We were mostly in Stockholm and New York, Merle."

"Oh, were you? So many years went by when you never bothered to write to me that I really can't keep pace. I thought about you a lot, of course. I want you to know you really had my sympathy, moving house all the time and that awful divorce from what's-his-name, and babies to cope with and then getting married again and everything. I used to feel how sad it was that I'd made so much of my life while you . . . What's the matter?"

"That plant, Merle, it moved."

"That's because you touched it. When you touch one of its mouths it closes up. It's called *Dionaea muscipula*."

The plant stood alone in a majolica pot contained in an elaborate white stand. It looked very healthy. It had delicate shiny leaves and from its heart grew five red-gold blossoms. As Daphne peered more closely she saw that these resembled mouths, as Merle had put it, far more than flowers, whiskery mouths, soft and ripe and luscious. One of these was now closed.

"Doesn't it have a common name?"

"Of course it does. The Venus' Fly-trap. *Muscipula* means fly-eater, dear."

"Whatever *do* you mean?"

"It eats flies. I've been trying to grow one for years. I was absolutely thrilled when I succeeded."

"Yes, but what d'you mean, it eats flies? It's not an animal."

"It is in a way, dear. The trouble is there aren't many flies here. I feed it on little bits of meat. You've gone rather pale, Daphne. Have you got a headache? We'll have our sherry now and then I'll see if I can catch a fly and you can see it eat it up."

"I'd really much rather not, Merle," said Daphne, backing away from the plant. "I don't want to hurt your feelings but I don't—well, I hate the idea of catching free live things and feeding them to—to that."

"*Free live things?* We're talking about flies." Merle, large and perfumed, grabbed Daphne's arm and pulled her away. Her dress was of red chiffon with trailing sleeves and her fingernails matched it. "The trouble with you," said Merle, "is that you're a mass of nerves and you're much worse now than you were when we were girls. I thank God every day of my life I don't know what it is to be neurotic. Here you are, your sherry. I've put it in a big glass to buck you up. I'm going to make it my business to look after you, Daphne. You don't know anybody else in London, do you?"

"Hardly anybody," said Daphne, sitting down where she couldn't see the Venus' Fly-trap. "My boys are in the States and my daughter's in Scotland."

"Well, you must come up here every day. No, you won't be intruding. When I first knew you were definitely coming I said to myself, I'm going to see to it Daphne isn't lonely. But don't imagine you'll get on with the other tenants in this block. Those of them who aren't standoffish snobs are—well, not the sort of people you'd want to know. But we won't talk about them. We'll talk about us. Unless, of course, you feel your past has been too painful to talk about?"

"I wouldn't quite say . . ."

"No, you wouldn't care to rake up unpleasant memories. I'll just put a drop more sherry in your glass and then I'll tell you all about my last venture, my agency."

Daphne rested her head against a cushion, brushed away an ivy frond, and prepared to listen.

From a piece of fillet steak Merle was scraping slivers of meat. She was all in diaphanous gold today, an amber chain around her neck, the finery half-covered by a frilly apron.

"I used to do that for my babies when they first went on solids," said Daphne.

"Babies, babies. You're always on about your babies. You've been up here every day for three weeks now and I don't think you've once missed an opportunity to talk about your babies and your men. Oh, I'm sorry, dear, I don't mean to upset you, but one really does get so weary of women like you talking about that side of life as if one had actually *missed* something."

"Why are you scraping that meat, Merle?"

"To feed my little Venus. That's her breakfast. Come along.

I've got a fly I caught under a sherry glass but I couldn't catch more than one."

The fly was very small. It was crawling up the inside of the glass, but when Merle approached it, it began to fly and buzz frenziedly against the transparent dome of its prison. Daphne turned her back. She went to the window, the huge, plant-filled bay window, and looked out, pretending to be interested in the view. She heard the scrape of glass and from Merle a triumphant gasp. Merle trod very heavily. Under the thick carpet the boards creaked. Merle began talking to the plant in a very gentle, maternal voice.

"This really is a wonderful outlook," said Daphne brightly, "You can see for miles."

Merle said, *"C'est Vénus toute entière à sa proie attachée."*

"I beg your pardon?"

"You never were any good at languages, dear. Oh, don't pretend you're so mad about that view. You're just being absurdly sensitive about what really amounts to *gardening*. I can't bear that sort of dishonesty. I've finished now, anyway. She's had her breakfast and all her mouths are shut up. Who are you waving to?"

"A rather nice young couple who live in the flat next to me."

"Well, please don't." Merle looked down and then drew herself up, all golden pleats and stiff golden curls. "You couldn't know, dear, but those two people are the very end. For one thing, they're not a couple, they're not married, I'm sure of that. Of course, that's no business of mine. What is my business is that they've been keeping a dog here—look, that spaniel thing—and it's strictly against the rules to keep animals in these flats."

"What about your Fly-trap?"

"Oh, don't be so silly! As I was saying, they keep that dog and let it foul the garden. I wrote to the managing agents, but those agents are so lax—they've no respect for me because I'm a single woman, I suppose. But I wrote again the day before yesterday and now I understand they're definitely going to be turned out."

Forty feet below the window, on the parking space between the block and the garden, the boy, who wore jeans and a leather jacket, picked up his dog and placed it on the back seat of a battered car. His companion, who had waist-length hair much the colour of Merle's dress, got into the passenger seat, but the boy hesitated. As Merle brought her face close to the glass, he looked up and raised two wide-splayed fingers.

"Oaf!" said Merle. "The only thing to do with people like that is to ignore them. Can you imagine it, he lets that dog of his relieve itself up against a really beautiful specimen of *Cryptomeria japonica*. Let's forget him and have a nice cup of coffee."

"Merle, how long will those flowers last on that Venus thing of yours? I mean, they'll soon die away, won't they?"

"No, they won't. They'll last for ages. You know, Daphne, fond as I am of you, I wouldn't leave you alone in this flat for anything. You've a personal hatred of my muscipula. You'd like to destroy it."

"I'll put the coffee on," said Daphne.

Merle phoned for a taxi. Then she put her little red address book with all the phone numbers in it into her scarlet patent-leather handbag along with her lipstick and her gold compact and her keys, her cheque book, and four five-pound notes.

"We could have walked," said Daphne.

"No, we couldn't, dear. When I have a day at the shops I like to feel fresh. I don't want to half-kill myself walking there. It's not the cost that's worrying you, is it? Because you know I'll pay. I appreciate the difference between our incomes, Daphne, and if I don't harp on it it's only because I try to be tactful. I want to buy you something, something really nice to wear. It seems such a wicked shame to me those men of yours didn't see to it you were well-provided for."

"I've got quite enough clothes, Merle."

"Yes, but all grey and black. The only bright thing you've got is that red hat and you've stopped wearing that."

"I'm old, Merle dear. I don't want to get myself up in bright colours. I've had my life."

"Well, I haven't had mine! I mean, I . . ." Merle bit her lip, getting scarlet lipstick on her teeth. She walked across the room, picked her ocelot coat off the back of the sofa, and paused in front of the Fly-trap. Its soft, flame-coloured mouths were open. She tickled them with her fingertips and they snapped shut. Merle giggled. "You know what you remind me of, Daphne? A fly. That's just what you look like in your grey coat and that funny bit of veil on your hat. A fly."

"There's the taxi," said Daphne.

It deposited them outside a large overheated store. Merle dragged Daphne through the jewellery department, the perfumery, past rotary stands with belts on them, plastic models in lingerie. They went up in the lift. Merle bought a model dress, orange chiffon with sequins on the skirt. They went down in the lift and into the next store. Merle bought face bracer and cologne and a gilt choker. They went up the escalator. Merle bought a brass link belt and tried to buy Daphne a green and blue silk scarf. Daphne consented at last to be presented with a pair of stockings, power elastic ones for her veins.

"Now we'll have lunch on the roof garden," said Merle.

"I should like a cup of tea."

"And I'll have a large sherry. But first I must freshen up. I'm dying to spend a penny and do my face."

They queued with their pennies. The ladies' cloakroom had green marble dressing tables with mirrors all down one side and green washbasins all down the other. Daphne sat down. Her feet had begun to swell. There were twenty or thirty other women in the cloakroom, doing their faces, resticking false eyelashes. One girl, whose face seemed vaguely familiar, was actually brushing her long golden hair. Merle put her handbag down on a free bit of green marble. She washed her hands, helped herself to a gush of Calèche from the scent-squirting machine, came back, opening and shutting her coat to fan herself. It was even hotter than in her flat.

She sat down, drew her chair to the mirror.

"Where's my handbag?" Merle screamed. "I left my handbag here! Someone's stolen my handbag. Daphne, Daphne, someone's stolen my handbag!"

The oyster satin sofa sagged under Merle's weight. Daphne smoothed back the golden curls and put another pad of cottonwool soaked in cologne on the red corrugated forehead.

"Bit better now?"

"I'm quite all right. I'm not one of your neurotic women to get into a state over a thing like that. Thank God I'd left my spare key with the porter and I hadn't locked the mortice."

"You'll have to have both locks changed, Merle."

"Of course I will, eventually. I'll see to it next week. Nobody can get in here, can they? They don't know who I am. I mean, they don't know whose keys they've got."

"They've got your handbag."

"Daphne dear, I do wish you wouldn't keep stating the obvious. *I know they have got my handbag*. The point is, there was nothing in my handbag to show who I am."

"There was your cheque book with your name on it."

"My name, dear, in case it's escaped your notice, is M. Smith. I haven't gone about changing it all my life like you." Merle sat up and took a gulp of walnut-brown sherry. "The store manager was charming, wasn't he, and the police? I daresay they'll find it, you know. It's a most distinctive handbag, not like that great black thing you cart about with you. My little red one could have gone inside yours. I wish I'd thought to put it there."

"I wish you had," said Daphne.

Daphne's phone rang. It was half past nine and she was finishing her breakfast, sitting in front of her little electric fire.

Merle sounded very excited. "What do you think? Isn't it marvellous? The store manager's just phoned to say they've found my bag. Well, it wasn't him, it was his secretary, stupid-sounding woman with one of those put-on accents. However, that's no concern of mine. They found my bag fallen down behind a radiator in that cloakroom. Isn't it an absolute miracle? Of course the money had gone, but my cheque book was there and the keys. I'm very glad I didn't take your advice and change those locks yesterday. It never does to act on impulse, Daphne."

"No, I suppose not."

"I've arranged to go down and collect my bag at eleven. As soon as I ring off, I'm going to phone for a taxi and I want you to come with me, dear. I'll have a bath and see to my plants— I've managed to catch a bluebottle for Venus—and then the taxi will be here."

"I'm afraid I can't come," said Daphne.

"Why on earth not?"

Daphne hesitated. Then she said, "I said I hardly know anybody in London but I do know this one man, this—well, he was a friend of my second husband, and he's a widower now and he's coming to lunch with me, Merle. He's coming at twelve and I must be here to see to things."

"A *man*?" said Merle. "*Another* man?"

"I'll look out for your taxi and when I see you come in I'll just pop up and hear all about it, shall I? I'm sorry I can't . . ."

"Sorry? Sorry for what? I can collect my handbag by myself. I'm quite used to standing on my own feet." The receiver went down with a crash.

Merle had a bath and put on the orange dress. It was rather showy for day wear with its sequins and its fringes, but she could never bear to have a new dress and not wear it at once. The ocelot coat would cover most of it. She watered the peperomias and painted a little leaf gloss on the ivy. The bluebottle had died in the night, but *Dionaea muscipula* didn't seem to mind. She opened her orange strandy mouths for Merle and devoured the dead bluebottle along with the shreds of fillet steak.

Merle put on her cream silk turban and a long scarf of flame-coloured silk. Her spare mortice key was where she always kept it, underneath the sanseveria pot. She locked the Yale and the mortice and then the taxi took her to the store. Merle sailed into the manager's office, and when the manager told her he had no secretary, had never phoned her flat, and had certainly not found her handbag, she deflated like a fat orange balloon into which someone has stuck a pin.

"You've been the victim of a hoax, Miss Smith."

Merle pulled herself together. She could always do that, she had superb control. She didn't want aspirins or brandy or policemen or any of the other aids to quietude offered by the manager. When she had told him he didn't know his job, that if there was a conspiracy against her—as she was sure there must be—he was in it, she floundered down the stairs and flapped her mouth and her arms for a taxi.

When she got home the first thing that struck her as strange was that the door was only locked on the Yale. She could have sworn she had locked it on the mortice too, but no doubt her memory was playing her tricks—and no wonder, the shock she had had. There was a little bit of earth on the hall carpet. Merle didn't like that, earth on her gold Wilton. Inside her ocelot she was sweating. She took off her coat and opened the drawing-room door.

Daphne saw the taxi come and Merle bounce out of it, an orange orchid springing from a black bandbox. Merle looked wild with excitement, her turban all askew. Daphne smiled to herself and shook her head. She laid the table and finished making the salad she knew her friend would like with his lunch, and then she went upstairs to see Merle.

There was a mirror on each landing. Daphne was so small and thin that she didn't puff much when she had to climb stairs. As she came to the top of each flight she saw a little grey woman trotting to meet her, a woman with smooth white hair and large, rather diffident grey eyes, who wore a grey wool dress partly covered by a cloudy stole of lace. She smiled at her reflection. She was old now but she had had her moments, her joy, her gratification, her intense pleasures. And soon there was to be a new pleasure, a confrontation she had looked forward to for weeks. Who could tell what would come of it? With a last smile at her grey and fluttery image, Daphne pushed open the unlatched door of Merle's flat.

In the Garden of Eden, the green paradisal bower, someone had dropped a bomb. No, they couldn't have done that, for the ceiling was still there and the carpet and the oyster satin furniture, torn now and plastered all over with earth. Every plant had been broken and torn apart. Leaves lay scattered in heaps like the leaves of autumn, only these were green, succulent, bruised. In the rape of the room, in the midst of ripped foliage, stems bleeding sap, shards of china, lay the Venus' Fly-trap, its roots wrenched from their pot and its mouths closed for ever.

Merle tried to scream but the noise came out only as a gurgle, the glug-glug agonised gasp of a scream in a nightmare. She fell on her knees and crawled about. Choking and muttering, she scrabbled among the earth and, picking up torn leaves, tried to piece them together like bits of a jigsaw puzzle. She crouched over the Fly-trap and nursed it in her hands, keening and swaying to and fro.

She didn't hear the door click shut. It was a long time before she realised Daphne was standing over her, silent, looking down. Merle lifted her red, streaming face. Daphne had her hand over her mouth, the hand with the two wedding rings on it. Merle thought Daphne must be covering her mouth to stop herself from laughing out loud.

Slowly, heavily, she got up. Her long orange scarf was in her hands, stretched taut, twisting, twisting. She was surprised how steady her voice was, how level and sane.

"You did it," she said. "You did it. You stole my handbag and took my keys and got me out of here and came in and did it."

Daphne quivered and shook her head. Her whole body shook and her hand flapped against her mouth. Quite whom Merle began to talk to then she didn't know, to herself or to Daphne, but she knew that what she said was true.

"You were so jealous! You'd had nothing, but I'd had success and happiness and love." Her voice went up and the scarf with it. "How you hated me, hated, hated . . . !" Merle screamed. "Hate, hate, poisonous jealous hate!" Huge and red and frondy, she descended on Daphne, engulfing her with musky orange petals, twisting the scarf round the frail insect neck, devouring the fly until the fly quivered into stillness.

An elderly man in a black homburg hat crossed the forecourt and went up the steps, a bunch of flowers in his hand. The boy in the leather jacket took no notice of him. He blushed earth and bits of leaf off his hands and said to the girl with the long hair, "Revenge is sweet." Then he tossed the scarlet handbag into the back of his car and he and the girl and the dog got in and drove away.

His Worst Enemy

The girl was hanging by her hands from the railings of a balcony. The balcony was on the twelfth floor of the high-rise block next to his. His flat was on the ninth floor and he had to look up to see her. It was half past six in the morning. He had been awakened by the sound of an aircraft flying dangerously low overhead, and had got out of bed to look. His sleepy gaze, descending from the blue sky, which was empty of clouds, empty of anything but the bright vanishing arrow of the aircraft, alighted—at first with disbelief—on the hanging figure.

He really thought he must be dreaming, for this sunrise time was the hour for dreams. Then, when he knew he wasn't, he decided it must be a stunt. This was to be a scene in a film. There were cameramen down there, a whole film unit, and all the correct safety precautions had been taken. Probably the girl wasn't even a real girl, but a dummy. He opened the window and looked down. The car park, paved courts, grass spaces between the blocks, all were deserted. On the balcony rail one of the dummy's hands moved, clutching its anchorage more tightly, more desperately. He had to believe then what was obviously happening—unbelievable only because melodrama, though a frequent constituent of real life, always is. The girl was trying to kill herself. She had lost her nerve and now was trying to stay alive. All these thoughts and conclusions of his occupied about thirty seconds. Then he acted. He picked up the phone and dialled the emergency number for the police.

The arrival of the police cars and the ultimate rescue of the girl became the focus of gossip and speculation for the tenants of the two blocks. Someone found out that it was he who had alerted the police and he became an unwilling hero. He was a modest, quiet young man, and, disliking this limelight, was relieved when the talk began to die away, when the novelty of it wore off, and he was able to enter and leave his flat without being pointed at as a kind of Saint George and sometimes even congratulated.

About a fortnight after that morning of melodrama, he was getting ready to go to the theatre, just putting on his overcoat, when the doorbell rang. He didn't recognise the girl who stood outside. He had never seen her face.

She said, "I'm Lydia Simpson. You saved my life. I've come to thank you."

His embarrassment was acute. "You shouldn't have," he said with a nervous smile. "You really shouldn't. That's not necessary. I only did what anyone would have done."

She was calm and tranquil, not at all his idea of a failed suicide. "But no one else did," she said.

"Won't you come in? Have a drink or something?"

"Oh, no, I couldn't think of it. I can see you're just going out. I only wanted to say thank you very, very much."

"It was nothing."

"Nothing to save someone's life? I'll always be grateful to you."

He wished she would either come in or go away. If this went on much longer the people in the other two flats on his floor would hear, would come out, and another of those bravest-deeds-of-the-year committee meetings would be convened. "Nothing at all," he said desperately. "Really, I've almost forgotten it."

"I shall never forget, never."

Her manner, calm yet intense, made him feel uncomfortable and he watched her retreat into the lift—smiling pensively—with profound relief. Luckily, they weren't likely to meet again. The curious thing was that they did, the next morning at the bus stop. She didn't refer again to his saving of her life, but talked instead about her new job, the reason for her being at this bus stop, at this hour. It appeared that her employers had offices in the City street next to his own and were clients of his own firm. They travelled to work together. He left her with very different feelings from those of the evening before. It was hard to believe she was thirty—his neighbours had given him this information—for she looked much younger, small and fragile as she was, her skin very white and her hair very fair.

They got into the habit of travelling on that bus together in the mornings, and sometimes she waved to him from her balcony. One evening they met by chance outside her office. She was carrying an armful of files to work on at home and confessed she wouldn't have brought them if she had known how heavy they were. Of course he carried them for her all the way up to her flat and stayed for a drink. She said she was going to cook dinner and would he stay for that too? He stayed. While she was out in the kitchen he took his drink out on to the balcony. It gave him a strange feeling, imagining her coming out here in her despair at dawn, lowering herself from those railings, then losing her nerve, beneath her a great space with death at the bottom of it. When she came back into the room, he noticed afresh how slight and frail she was, how in need of protection.

The flat was neat and spotlessly clean. Most of the girls he knew lived in semi-squalor. Liberated, independent creatures, holding down men's jobs, they scorned womanly skills as debasing. He had been carefully brought up by a houseproud mother and he liked a clean home. Lydia's furniture was beautifully polished. He thought that if he were ever asked again he would remember to bring her flowers to go in those sparkling glass vases.

After dinner, an excellent, even elaborate meal, he said suddenly, the food and drink lowering his inhibitions, "Why did you do it?"

"Try to kill myself?" She spoke softly and evenly, as serenely as if he had asked why she changed her job. "I was engaged and he left me for someone else. There didn't seem much to live for."

"Are you over that now?"

"Oh, yes. I'm glad I didn't succeed. Or—should I say?—that you didn't let me succeed."

"Don't ever try that again, will you?"

"No, why should I? What a question!"

He felt strangely happy that she had promised never to try that again. "You must come and have a meal with me," he said as he was leaving. "Let's see. Not Monday. How about . . . ?"

"We don't have to arrange it now, do we? We'll see each other in the morning."

She had a very sweet smile. He didn't like aggressive, self-reliant women. Lydia never wore trousers or mini-dresses, but long flowing skirts, flower-patterned. When he put his hand under her elbow to shepherd her across the street, she clutched his arm and kept hold of it.

"You choose for me," she said when the menu was given to her in the restaurant.

She didn't smoke or drink anything stronger than sweet white wine. She couldn't drive a car. He wondered sometimes how she managed to hold down an exacting job, pay her rent, live alone. She was so exquisitely feminine, clinging and gentle. And he was flattered when because of the firm's business he was unable to see her one night, tears appeared in her large grey eyes. That was the first night they hadn't met for three weeks and he missed her so much he knew he must be in love with her.

She accepted his proposal, made formally and accompanied by a huge bunch of red roses. "Of course I'll marry you. My life has been yours ever since you saved it. I've always felt I belonged to you."

They were married very quietly. Lydia didn't like the idea of a big wedding. He and she were ideally suited, they had so many tastes in common: a love of quietness and order, rather old-fashioned ways, steadiness, regular habits. They had the same aims: a house in a north-western suburb, two children. But for the time being she would continue to work.

It amazed and delighted him that she managed to keep the new house so well, to provide him every morning with freshly laundered underwear and shirt, every night with a perfectly cooked meal. He hadn't been so well looked after since he had left his mother's house. That, he thought, was how a woman should be, unobtrusively efficient, gentle yet expert, feminine and sweet, yet accomplished. The house was run as smoothly as if a couple of silent, invisible maids were at work in it all day.

To perform these chores, she got up each morning at six. He suggested they get a cleaner but she wouldn't have one, resisting him without defiance but in a way which was bound to appeal to him.

"I couldn't bear to let any other woman look after your things, darling."

She was quite perfect.

They went to work together, lunched together, came home together, ate together, watched television or listened to music or read in companionable silence together, slept together. At the weekends they were together all the time. Both had decided their home must be fully equipped with washers and driers and freezers and mixers and cleaners and polishers, beautifully furnished with the brand-new or the extreme antique, so on Saturdays they shopped together.

He adored it. This was what marriage should be, this was what the church service meant—one flesh, forsaking all other. He had, in fact, forsaken most of the people he had once known. Lydia wasn't a very sociable woman and had no women friends. He asked her why not.

"Women," she said, "only want to know other women to gossip about their men. I haven't any complaints against my man, darling."

His own friends seemed a little overawed by the grandeur and pomp with which she entertained them, by the finger bowls and fruit knives. Or perhaps they were put off by her long silences and the way she kept glancing at her watch. It was only natural, of course, that she didn't want people staying half the night. She wanted to be alone with him. They might have understood that and made allowances. His clients and their wives weren't overawed. They must have been gratified. Where else, in a private house with no help, would they have been given a five-course dinner, exquisitely cooked and served? Naturally, Lydia had to spend all the pre-dinner time in the kitchen and, naturally too, she was exhausted after dinner, a little snappy with the man who spilt coffee on their new carpet, and the other one, a pleasant if tactless stockbroker, who tried to persuade him to go away on a stag, golfing weekend.

"Why did they get married," she asked, with some reason, "if all they want to do is get away from their wives?"

By this time, at the age of thirty-four, he ought to have had promotion at work. He'd been with the firm five years and expected to be made a director. Neither he nor Lydia could understand why this directorship was so slow in coming.

"I wonder," he said, "if it's because I don't hang around in the office drinking after work?"

"Surely they understand a married man wants to be with his wife?"

"God knows. Maybe I ought to have gone on that river-boat party, only wives weren't invited, if you remember. I could tell you were unhappy at the idea of my going alone."

In any case, he'd probably been quite wrong about the reason for his lack of promotion because, just as he was growing really worried about it, he got his directorship. An increase in salary, an office, and a secretary of his own. He was a little concerned about other perquisites of the job, particularly about the possibility of foreign trips. But there was no need to mention these to Lydia yet. Instead he mentioned the secretary he must engage.

"That's marvellous, darling." They were dining out, tête-à-tête, to celebrate. Lydia hadn't cared for his idea of a party. "I'll have to give a fortnight's notice, but you can wait a fortnight, can't you? It'll be lovely being together all day long."

"I don't quite follow," he said, though he did.

"Darling, you are slow tonight. Where could you find a better secretary than me?"

They had been married for four years. "You're going to give up work and have a baby."

She took his hand, smiling into his face. "That can wait. We don't need children to bring us together. You're my husband and my child and my friend all in one, and that's enough for me."

He had to tell her why it wouldn't do for her to be his secretary. It was all true, that stuff about office politics and favouritism and the awkwardness of his position if his wife worked for him, but he made a poor show of explaining.

She said in her small, soft voice, "Please can we go? Could you ask them for the bill? I'd like to leave now."

As soon as they were in the house she began to cry. He advanced afresh his explanation. She cried. He said she could ask other people. Everyone would tell her the same. A director of a small firm like his couldn't have his wife working for him. She could phone his chairman if she didn't believe him.

She didn't raise her voice. She was never wild or hysterical. "You don't want me," she said like a rejected child.

"I do want you. I love you. But—can't you see—this is for work, this is different." He knew, before he said it, that he shouldn't have gone on. "You don't like my friends and I've given them up. I don't have my clients here any more. I'm only away from you about six hours out of every day. Isn't all that enough for you?"

There was no argument. She simply reiterated that he didn't want her. She cried for most of the night and in the morning she was too tired to go to work. During the day he phoned her twice. She sounded tearful but calm, apparently resigned now. The first thing he noticed when he let himself in at his front door at six was the stench of gas.

She was lying on the kitchen floor, a cushion at the edge of the open oven to support her delicate blonde head. Her face was flushed a warm pink.

He flung open the window and carried her to it, holding her head in the fresh air. She was alive, she would be all right. As her pulse steadied and she began to breathe more evenly, he found himself kissing her passionately, begging her aloud not to die, to live for him. When he thought it was safe to leave her for a moment, he laid her on the sofa and dialled the emergency number for an ambulance.

They kept her in hospital for a few days and there was talk of mental treatment. She refused to undergo it.

"I've never done it except when I've known I'm not loved," she said.

"What do you mean, 'never,' darling?"

"When I was seventeen I took an overdose of pills because a boy let me down."

"You never told me," he said.

"I didn't want to upset you. I'd rather die than make you unhappy. My life belongs to you and I only want to make yours happy."

Suppose he hadn't got there in time? He shuddered when he thought of that possibility. The house was horrible without her. He missed her painfully, and he resolved to devote more of his time and his attention to her in future.

She didn't like going away on holiday. Because they never took holidays and seldom entertained and had no children, they had been able to save. They sold the house and bought a bigger, newer one. His firm wanted him to go to Canada for three weeks and he didn't hesitate. He refused immediately.

An up-and-coming junior got the Canada trip. It irritated him when he learned of a rumour that was going about the office to the effect that his wife was some sort of invalid, just because she had given up work since they bought the new house. Lydia, an invalid? She was happier than she had ever been, filling the house with new things, redecorating rooms herself, having the garden landscaped. If either of them was sick, it was he. He hadn't been sleeping well lately and he became subject to fits of depression. The doctor gave him pills for the sleeplessness and advised a change of air. Perhaps he was working too hard. Couldn't he manage to do some of his work at home?

"I took it upon myself," Lydia said gently, "to phone the doctor and suggest that. You could have two or three days a week at home and I'd do the secretarial work for you."

His chairman agreed to it. There was a hint of scorn in the man's smile, he thought. But he was allowed to work at home and sometimes, for four or five days at a stretch, although he talked to people on the phone, he saw no one at all but his wife. She was, he found, as perfect a secretary as a wife. There was scarcely anything for him to do. She composed his press releases for him, wrote his letters without his having to dictate them, answered the phone with efficiency and charm, arranged his appointments. And she waited on him unflaggingly when work was done. No meals on trays for them. Every lunchtime and every evening the dining table was exquisitely laid, and if it occurred to him that in the past two years only six other people had handled this glass, this cutlery, these luxurious appointments, he didn't say so.

His depression wouldn't go away, even though he had tranquillisers now as well as sleeping pills. They never spoke of her suicide attempts, but he often thought of them and wondered if he had somehow been infected by this tendency of hers. When, before settling down for the night, he dropped one pill from the bottle into the palm of his hand, the temptation to let them all trickle out, to swallow them all down with a draught of fresh cold water, was sometimes great. He didn't know why, for he had everything a man could want, a perfect marriage, a beautiful house, a good job, excellent physical health, and no ties or restrictions.

As Lydia had pointed out, "Children would have been such a tie, darling," or, when he suggested they might buy a dog, "Pets are an awful tie, and they ruin one's home." He agreed that this home and these comforts were what he had always wanted. Yet, as he approached forty, he began having bad dreams, and the dreams were of prisons.

One day he said to her, "I can understand now why you tried to kill yourself. I mean, I can understand that anyone might want to."

"I think we understand each other perfectly in every way," she said. "But don't let's talk about it. I'll never attempt it again."

"And I'm not the suicidal type, am I?"

"*You?*" She wasn't alarmed, she didn't take him seriously, never thought of him at all as a person except in relation to herself. At once he reproached himself. *Lydia?* Lydia, who had given over her whole life to him, who put his every need and wish before her own? "You wouldn't have any reason to," she said gaily. "You know you're loved. Besides, I should rescue you in time, just like you rescued me."

His company had expanded and they were planning to open an office in Melbourne. After he had denied hotly that his wife was an invalid, that there was "some little trouble" with his wife, the chairman offered him the chance of going to Australia for three months to get the new branch on its feet. Again he didn't hesitate. He accepted. The firm would, of course, pay for his trip. He was working out, as he entered his house, how much Lydia's air fare to Melbourne, her board in an hotel, her expenses, would amount to. Suicidal thoughts retreated. He could do it, he could just do it. Three months away, he thought, in a new country, meeting new people, and at the end of it, praise for his work and maybe an increase in salary.

She came out into the hall and embraced him. Her embraces at parting and greeting (though these occasions were no longer frequent) were as passionate now as when they first got engaged. He anticipated a small difficulty in that she wouldn't much want to leave her home, but that could be got over. She would go, as she had often said, anywhere with him.

He walked into their huge living room. It was as immaculate as ever, but something was different, something had undergone a great change. Their red carpet had been replaced by a new one of a delicate creamy velvety pile.

"Do you like it?" she asked, smiling. "I bought it and had it laid secretly as a surprise for you. Oh, darling, you don't like it?"

"I like it," he said, and then, "How much did it cost?"

This was a question he hardly ever asked, but now he had cause to. She named a sum, much about the figure her trip to Australia would have cost.

"We said we were saving it to get something for the house," she said, putting her arm round him. "It's not really an extravagance. It'll last for ever. And what else have we got to spend the money on but our own home?"

He kissed her and said it didn't matter. It wasn't really an extravagance and it would last for ever, for ever. . . .

They dined off Copenhagen china and Georgian silver and Waterford glass. On the table flowers were arranged, wasting their sweetness on the desert air. He must go to Australia, but she couldn't come with him. He was afraid to tell her, gripped by a craven fear.

For weeks he put off telling her, and treacherously the idea came to him—why tell her at all? He longed to go, he must go. Couldn't he simply escape, phone her from the aircraft's first stop, somewhere in Europe, and say he had been sent without notice, urgently? He had tried to phone her before but he couldn't get through. She wouldn't attempt suicide, he was sure, if she knew he was too far away to save her. And she'd forgive him, she loved him. But there were too many practical difficulties in the way of that, clothes, for instance, luggage. He must have been losing his mind even to think of it. Do that to *Lydia*? He wouldn't do that to his worst enemy, still less to his beloved wife.

As it turned out, he didn't get the chance. She was his secretary from whom a man, however many he keeps from his wife, can have no secrets. The airline phoned with a query and she found out.

"How long," she asked dully, "will you be gone?"

"Three months."

She paled. She fell back as if physically ill.

"I'll write every day. I'll phone."

"Three months," she said.

"I was scared stiff of telling you. I have to go. Darling, don't you see I have to? It would cost hundreds and hundreds to take you with me, and we don't have the money."

"No," she said. "No, of course not."

She cried bitterly that night but on the following morning

she didn't refer to his departure. They worked together as efficiently and companionable as ever, but her face was paper-white. Work finished, she began to talk of the clothes he would need, the new suitcases to be bought. In a sad, monotonous voice, she said that she would do everything, he mustn't worry his head at all about preparations.

"And you won't worry about *me* on the flight?"

There was something about the way she said she wouldn't, shaking her head and smiling as if his question had been pre-posterous, unreal, that told him. The dead cannot worry. She intended to be dead. And he understood that he had been ab-surdly optimistic in reassuring himself she wouldn't attempt suicide when he was far away.

The days went by. Only one more before he was due to leave. But he wouldn't leave. He knew that. He had known it for more than a week, and he was as afraid of telling his chair-man he wouldn't as he had been afraid of telling her he would. Again he dreamed of prisons. He awoke to see his life as an al-ternating between fear and captivity, fear and imprison-ment. . . .

The escape route from both was available. It was on the af-ternoon of the last day that he decided to take it. He had told neither his wife nor his chairman that he wasn't going to Aus-tralia, and everything was packed, his luggage arranged in the hall with a precision of which only Lydia was capable. She had told him she was going out to fetch his best lightweight suit from the cleaners, the suit he was to wear on the following day, and he had heard the front door close.

That had been half an hour before. While she was out he was to go upstairs, she had instructed him sadly and tenderly, and check that there was no vital item she had left unpacked. And at last he went, but for another purpose. A lethal, not a vital, item was what he wanted—the bottle of sleeping pills.

The bedroom door was closed. He opened it and saw her lying on their bed. She hadn't gone out. For half an hour she had been lying there, the empty bottle of pills still clutched feebly in her hand. He felt her pulse, and a firm but unsteady flicker passed into his fingers. She was alive. Another quarter of an hour, say, and the ambulance would have her in hospital. He reached for the phone extension and put his finger to the slot to dial the emergency number. She'd be saved. Thank God, once again, he wasn't too late.

He looked down at her peaceful, tranquil face. She looked no older than on that day when she had come to him to thank him for saving her life. Gradually, almost involuntarily, he withdrew his finger from the dial. A heavy sob almost choked him and he heard himself give a whimpering cry. He lifted her in his arms, kissing her passionately and speaking her name aloud over and over again.

Then he walked quickly out of that room and out of the house. A bus came. He got on it and bought a ticket to some distant, outlying suburb. There, in a park he didn't know and had never visited, he lay on the grass and fell into a deep sleep.

When he awoke it was nearly dark. He looked at his watch and saw that more than enough time had passed. Wiping his eyes, for he had apparently cried in his sleep, he got up and went home.

The Vinegar Mother

All this happened when I was eleven.

Mop Felton was at school with me and she was supposed to be my friend. I say "supposed to be" because she was one of those close friends all little girls seem to have yet don't very much like. I had never liked Mop. I knew it then just as I know it now, but she was my friend because she lived in the next street, was the same age, in the same form, and because my parents, though not particularly intimate with the Feltons, would have it so.

Mop was a nervous, strained, dramatic creature, in some ways old for her age and in others very young. Hindsight tells me that she had no self-confidence but much self-esteem. She was an only child who flew into noisy rages or silent huffs when teased. She was tall and very skinny and dark, and it wasn't her hair, thin and lank, which accounted for her nickname. Her proper name was Alicia. I don't know why we called her Mop, and if now I see in it some obscure allusion to mopping and mowing (a Shakespearean description which might have been associated with her) or in the monosyllable the hint of a witch's familiar (again, not inept), I am attributing to us an intellectual sophistication which we didn't possess.

We were gluttons for nicknames. Perhaps all schoolgirls are. But there was neither subtlety nor finesse in our selection. Margaret myself, I was dubbed Margarine. Rhoda Joseph, owing to some gagging and embarrassment during a public recitation of Wordsworth, was for ever after Lucy; Elizabeth Goodwin was Goat because this epithet had once been applied to her by higher authority on the hockey field. Our nicknames were not exclusive, being readily interchangeable with our true christian names at will. We never used them in the presence of parent or teacher and they, if they had known of them, would not have deigned use them to us. It was, therefore, all the more astonishing to hear them from the lips of Mr Felton, the oldest and richest of any of our fathers.

Coming home from work into a room where Mop and I were: "How's my old Mopsy, then?" he would say, and to me, "Well, it's jolly old Margarine!"

I used to giggle, as I always did when confronted by something mildly embarrassing that I didn't understand. I was an observant child but not sensitive. Children, in any case, are little given to empathy. I can't recall that I ever pitied Mop for having a father who, though over fifty, pretended too often to be her contemporary. But I found it satisfactory that my own father, at her entry, would look up vaguely from his book and mutter, "Hallo—er, Alicia, isn't it?"

The Feltons were on a slightly higher social plane than we, a fact I did know and accepted without question and without resentment. Their house was bigger, each parent possessed a car, they ate dinner in the evenings. Mr Felton used to give Mop half a glass of sherry to drink.

"I don't want you growing up ignorant of wine," he would say.

And if I were present I would get the sherry too. I suppose it was Manzanilla, for it was very dry and pale yellow, the colour of the stone in a ring Mrs Felton wore which entirely hid her wedding ring.

They had a cottage in the country where they went at the weekends and sometimes for the summer holidays. Once they took me there for a day. And the summer after my eleventh birthday, Mr Felton said: "Why don't you take old Margarine with you for the holidays?"

It seems strange now that I should have wanted to go. I had a very happy childhood, a calm, unthinking, unchanging relationship with my parents and my brothers. I liked Rhoda and Elizabeth far more than I liked Mop, whose rages and fantasies and sulks annoyed me, and I disliked Mrs Felton more than any grown-up I knew. Yet I did want to go very much. The truth was that even then I had begun to develop my passion for houses, the passion that has led me to become a designer of them, and one day in that cottage had been enough to make me love it. All my life had been spent in a semi-detached villa, circa 1935, in a London suburb. The Feltons' cottage, which had the pretentious (not to me, then) name of Sanctuary, was four hundred years old, thatched, half-timbered, of wattle and daub construction, a calendar-maker's dream, a chocolate-box artist's ideal. I wanted to sleep within those ancient walls, tread upon floors that had been there before the Armada came, press my face against glass panes that had reflected a ruff or a Puritan's starched collar.

My mother put up a little opposition. She liked me to know Mop, she also perhaps liked me to be associated with the Feltons' social cachet, but I had noticed before that she didn't much like me to be in the care of Mrs Felton.

"And Mr Felton will only be there at the weekends," she said.

"If Margaret doesn't like it," said my father, "she can write home and get us to send her a telegram saying you've broken your leg."

"Thanks very much," said my mother. "I wish you wouldn't teach the children habits of deception."

But in the end she agreed. If I were unhappy, I was to phone from the call box in the village and then they would write and say my grandmother wanted me to go and stay with her. Which, apparently, was not teaching me habits of deception.

In the event, I wasn't at all unhappy, and it was to be a while before I was even disquieted. There was plenty to do. It was fruit-growing country, and Mop and I picked fruit for Mr Gould, the farmer. We got paid for this, which Mrs Felton seemed to think *infra dig*. She didn't associate with the farmers or the agricultural workers. Her greatest friend was a certain Lady Elsworthy, an old woman whose title (I later learned she was the widow of a Civil Service knight) placed her in my estimation in the forefront of the aristocracy. I was stricken dumb whenever she and her son were at Sanctuary and much preferred the company of our nearest neighbour, a Mrs Potter, who was perhaps gratified to meet a juvenile enthusiast of architecture. Anyway, she secured for me the entrée to the Hall, a William and Mary mansion, through whose vast chambers I walked hand in hand with her, awed and wondering and very well content.

Sanctuary had a small parlour, a large dining-living room, a kitchen, and a bathroom on the ground floor and two bedrooms upstairs. The ceilings were low and sloping and so excessively beamed, some of the beams being carved, that were I to see it now I would probably think it vulgar, though knowing it authentic. I am sure that nowadays I would think the Feltons' furniture vulgar, for their wealth, such as it was, didn't run to the purchasing of true antiques. Instead, they had those piecrust tables and rent tables and little escritoires which, cunningly chipped and scratched in the right places, inlaid with convincingly scuffed and dimly gilded leather—maroon, olive, or amber—had been manufactured at a factory in Romford.

I knew this because Mr Felton, down for the weekend, would announce it to whomsoever might be present.

"And how old do you suppose that is, Lady Elsworthy?" he would say, fingering one of those deceitful little tables as he placed on it her glass of citrine-coloured sherry. "A hundred and fifty years? Two hundred?"

Of course she didn't know or was too well-bred to say.

"One year's your answer! Factory-made last year and I defy anyone but an expert to tell the difference."

Then Mop would have her half-glass of sherry and I mine while the adults watched us for the signs of intoxication they seemed to find so amusing in the young and so disgraceful in the old. And then dinner with red or white wine, but none for us this time. They always had wine, even when, as was often the case, the meal was only sandwiches or bits of cold stuff on toast. Mr Felton used to bring it down with him on Saturdays, a dozen bottles sometimes in a cardboard case. I wonder if it was good French wine or sour cheap stuff from Algeria that my father called plonk? Whatever Mr Felton's indulgence with the sherry had taught me, it was not to lose my ignorance of wine.

But wine plays a part in this story, an important part. For, as she sipped the dark red stuff in her glass, blood-black with—or am I imagining this?—a blacker scaling of lees in its depths, Lady Elsworthy said, "Even if you're only a moderate wine-drinker, my dear, you ought, you really ought, to have a vinegar mother."

On this occasion I wasn't the only person present to giggle. There were cries of "A *what?*" and some laughter and then Lady Elsworthy began an explanation of what a vinegar mother was, a culture of acetobacter that would convert wine into vinegar. Her son, whom the adults called Peter, supplied the technical details and the Potters asked questions and from time to time someone would say, "A vinegar mother! What a name!" I wasn't much interested and I wandered off into the garden, where, after a few minutes, Mop joined me. She was, as usual, carrying a book but instead of sitting down, opening the book and excluding me, which was her custom, she stood staring into the distance of the Stour Valley and the Weeping Hills—I think she leant against a tree—and her face had on it that protuberant-featured expression which heralded one of her rages. I asked her what was the matter.

"I've been sick."

I knew she hadn't been, but I asked her why.

"That horrible old woman and that horrible thing she was talking about, like a bit of liver in a bottle, she said." Her mouth trembled. "Why does she call it a vinegar *mother?*"

"I don't know," I said. "Perhaps because mothers make children and it makes vinegar."

That only seemed to make her angrier and she kicked at the tree.

"Shall we go down to the pond or are you going to read?" I said.

But Mop didn't answer me so I went down to the pond alone and watched the bats that flitted against a pale green sky. Mop had gone up to our bedroom. She was in bed reading when I got back. No reader myself, I remember the books she liked and remember too that my mother thought she ought not to be allowed to read them. That night it was Lefanu's *Uncle Silas* which engrossed her. She had just finished Dr James's *Ghost Stories of an Antiquary*. I don't believe, at that time, I saw any connection between her literary tastes and her reaction to the vinegar mother, nor did I attribute this latter to anything lacking in her relationship with her own mother. I couldn't have done so; I was much too young. I hadn't, anyway, been affected by the conversation at supper and I went to bed with no uneasy forebodings about what was to come.

In the morning when Mop and I came back from church—we were sent there, I now think, from a desire on the part of Mr and Mrs Felton to impress the neighbours rather than out of vicarious piety—we found the Elsworthys once more at Sanctuary. Lady Elsworthy and her son and Mrs Felton were all peering into a glass vessel with a narrow, stoppered mouth in which was some brown liquid with a curd floating on it. This curd did look quite a lot like a slice of liver.

"It's alive," said Mop. "It's a sort of animal."

Lady Elsworthy told her not to be a little fool and Mrs Felton laughed. I thought my mother would have been angry if a visitor to our house had told me not to be a fool, and I also thought Mop was really going to be sick this time.

"We don't have to have it, do we?" she said.

"Of course we're going to have it," said Mrs Felton. "How dare you speak like that when Lady Elsworthy has been kind enough to give it to me! Now we shall never have to buy nasty shop vinegar again."

"Vinegar doesn't cost much," said Mop.

"Isn't that just like a child! Money grows on trees as far as she's concerned."

Then Lady Elsworthy started giving instructions for the maintenance of the thing. It must be kept in a warm atmosphere. "Not out in your chilly kitchen, my dear." It was to be fed with wine, the dregs of each bottle they consumed. "But not white wine. You tell her why not, Peter; you know I'm no good at the scientific stuff." It must never be touched with a knife or metal spoon.

"If metal touches it," said Peter Elsworthy, "it will shrivel and die. In some ways, you see, it's a tender plant."

Mop had banged out of the room. Lady Elsworthy was once more bent over her gift, holding the vessel and placing it in a suitable position where it was neither too light nor too cold. From the garden I could hear the drone of the lawn mower, plied by Mr Felton. Those other two had moved a little away from the window, away from the broad shaft of sunshine in which we had found them bathed. As Peter Elsworthy spoke of the tender plant, I saw his eyes meet Mrs Felton's and there passed between them a glance, mysterious, beyond my comprehension, years away from anything I knew. His face became soft and strange. I wanted to giggle as I sometimes giggled in the cinema, but I knew better than to do so there, and I went away and giggled by myself in the garden, saying, "Soppy, soppy!" and kicking at a stone.

But I wasn't alone. Mr Felton came pushing the lawn mower up behind me. He used to sweat in the heat and his face was red and wet like the middle of a joint of beef when the brown part has been carved off. A grandfather rather than a father, I thought him.

"What's soppy, my old Margarine? Mind out of my way or I'll cut your tail off."

It was August and the season had begun, so on Sunday afternoons he would take the shotgun he kept hanging in the kitchen and go out after rabbits. I believe he did this less from a desire to eat rabbit flesh than from a need to keep in with the Elsworthys, who shot every unprotected thing that flew or scuttled. But he was a poor shot and I used to feel relieved when he came back empty-handed. On Sunday evenings he drove away to London.

"Poor old Daddy back to the grindstone," he would say. "Take care of yourself, my old Mop." And to me, with wit, "Don't melt away in all this sunshine, Margarine."

That Sunday Mrs Felton made him promise to bring a dozen more bottles of wine when he returned the following weekend.

"Reinforcements for my vinegar mother."

"It's stupid wasting wine to make it into vinegar," said Mop. I wondered why she used to hover so nervously about her parents at this leave-taking time, watching them both, her fists clenched. Now I know it was because, although she was rude to them and seemed not to care for them, she longed desperately to see them exchange some demonstration of affection greater than Mrs Felton's apathetic lifting of her cheek and the hungry peck Mr Felton deposited upon it. But she waited in vain, and when the car had gone would burst into a seemingly inexplicable display of ill-temper or sulks.

So another week began, a week in which our habits, until then routine and placid, were to change.

Like a proper writer, a professional, I have hinted at Mrs Felton and, I hope, whetted appetites, but I have delayed till now giving any description of her. But, having announced her entry through the mouths of my characters (as in all the best plays), I shall delay no more. The stage is ready for her and she shall enter it, in her robes and with her trumpets.

She was a tall, thin woman and her skin was as brown as a pale Indian's. I thought her old and very ugly, and I couldn't understand a remark of my mother's that I had overheard to the effect that Mrs Felton was "quite beautiful if you like that gypsy look." I suppose she was about thirty-seven or thirty-eight. Her hair was black and frizzy, like a bush of heather singed by fire, and it grew so low on her forehead that her black brows sprang up to meet it, leaving only an inch or so of skin between. She had a big mouth with brown thick lips she never painted and enormous eyes whose whites were like wet eggshells.

In the country she wore slacks and a shirt. She made some of her own clothes and those she made were dramatic. I remember a hooded cloak she had of brown hessian and a long evening gown of embroidered linen. At that time women seldom wore cloaks or long dresses, either for evening or day. She chain-smoked and her fingers were yellow with nicotine.

Me she almost entirely ignored. I was fed and made to wash properly and told to change my clothes and not allowed to be out after dark. But apart from this she hardly spoke to me. I think she had a ferocious dislike of children, for Mop fared very little better than I did. Mrs Felton was one of those women who fall into the habit of only addressing their children to scold them. However presentable Mop might make herself, however concentratedly good on occasion her behaviour—for I believe she made great efforts—Mrs Felton couldn't bring herself to praise. Or if she could, there would always be the sting in the tail, the "Well, but look at your nails!" or "It's very nice but do you have to pick this moment?" And Mop's name on her tongue—as if specifically chosen to this end—rang with a sour slither, a little green snake slipping from its hole, as the liquid and the sibilant scathed out, "Alicia!"

But at the beginning of that third week a slight change came upon her. She was not so much nicer or kinder as more vague, more nervously abstracted. Mop's peccadillos passed unnoticed and I, if late for a meal received no venomous glance. It was on the Tuesday evening that the first wine bottle appeared at our supper table.

We ate this meal, cold usually but more than a bread and butter tea, at half past seven or eight in the evening, and after it we were sent to bed. There had never before been the suggestion that we should take wine with it. Even at the weekends we were never given wine, apart from our tiny glasses of educative sherry. But that night at sunset—I remember the room all orange and quiet and warm—Mrs Felton brought to the table a bottle of red wine instead of the teapot and the lemon barley water, and set out three glasses.

"I don't like wine," said Mop.

"Yes, you do. You like sherry."

"I don't like that dark red stuff. It tastes bitter. Daddy won't let me have wine."

"Then we won't tell Daddy. If it's bitter you can put sugar in it. My God, any other child would think it was in heaven getting wine for supper. You don't know when you're well off and you never have. You've no appreciation."

"I suppose you want us to drink it so you can have the leftovers for your horrible vinegar thing," said Mop.

"It's not horrible and don't you dare to speak to me like that," said Mrs Felton, but there was something like relief in her voice. Can I remember that? Did I truly observe *that*? No. It is now that I know it, now when all the years have passed, and year by year has come more understanding. Then, I heard no relief. I saw no baser motive in Mrs Felton's insistence. I took it for granted, absurd and somehow an inversion of the proper course of things though it seemed, that we were to drink an expensive substance in order that the remains of it might be converted into a cheap substance. But childhood is a looking-glass country where so often one is obliged to believe six impossible things before breakfast.

I drank my wine and, grudgingly, Mop drank two full glasses into which she had stirred sugar. Most of the rest was consumed by Mrs Felton, who then poured the dregs into the glass vessel for the refreshment of the vinegar mother. I don't think I had ever drunk or even tasted table wine before. It went to my head, and as soon as I was in bed at nine o'clock I fell into a profound thick sleep.

But Mop was asleep before me. She had lurched into bed without washing and I heard her heavy breathing while I was pulling on my nightdress. This was unusual. Mop wasn't exactly an insomniac but, for a child, she was a bad sleeper. Most evenings as I was passing into those soft clouds of sleep, into a delightful drowsiness that at any moment would be closed off by total oblivion, I would hear her toss and turn in bed or even get up and move about the room. I knew, too, that sometimes she went downstairs for a glass of water or perhaps just for her mother's company, for on the mornings after such excursions Mrs Felton would take her to task over breakfast, scathingly demanding of invisible hearers why she should have been cursed with such a restless, nervy child, who, even as a baby, had never slept a peaceful night through.

On the Tuesday night, however, she had no difficulty in falling asleep. It was later, in the depths of the night (as she told me in the morning) that she had awakened and lain wakeful for hours, or so she said. She had heard the church clock chime two and three; her head had ached and she had had a curious trembling in her limbs. But, as far as I know, she said nothing of this to her mother, and her headache must have passed by the middle of the morning. For, when I left the house at ten to go with Mrs Potter to an auction that was being held in some neighbouring mansion, she was lying on a blanket on the front lawn, reading the book Mr Felton had brought down for her at the weekend, *Fifty Haunted Houses*. And she was still reading it, was deep in "The Mezzotint" or some horror of Blackwood's, when I got back at one.

It must have been that day, too, when she began to get what I should now call obsessional about the vinegar mother. Several times, three or four times certainly, when I went into the dining room, I found her standing by the Romford factory antique on which Lady Elsworthy's present stood, gazing with the fascination of someone who views an encapsulated reptile, at the culture within. It was not to me in any way noisome or sinister, nor was it even particularly novel. I had seen a dish of stewed fruit forgotten and allowed to ferment in my grandmother's larder, and apart from the fungus on that being pale green, there was little difference between it and this crust of bacteria. Mop's face, so repelled yet so compelled, made me giggle. A mistake, this, for she turned on me, lashing out with a thin wiry arm.

"Shut up, shut up! I hate you."

But she had calmed and was speaking to me again by suppertime. We sat on the wall above the road and watched Mr Gould's Herefords driven from their pasture up the lane home to the farm. Swallows perched on the telephone wires like taut strings of black and white beads. The sky was lemony-green and greater birds flew homeward across it.

"I'd like to put a spoon in it," said Mop, "and then I'd see it shrivel up and die."

"She'd know," I said.

"Who's she?"

"Your mother, of course." I was surprised at the question when the answer was so obvious. "Who else?"

"I don't know."

"It's only an old fungus," I said. "It isn't hurting you."

"Alicia! Aleeciah!" A sharp liquid cry, the sound of a sight, and the sight wine or vinegar flung in a curving jet.

"Come on, Margarine," said Mop. "Supper's ready."

We were given no wine that night, but on the next a bottle and the glasses once more appeared. The meal was a heavier one than usual, meat pie with potatoes as well as salad. Perhaps the wine was sweet this time or of a finer vintage, for it tasted good to me and I drank two glasses. It never occurred to me to wonder what my parents, moderate and very nearly abstemious, would have thought of this corruption of their daughter. Of course it didn't. To a child grown-ups are omniscient and all-wise. Much as I disliked Mrs Felton, I never supposed she could wish to harm me or be indifferent as to whether or not I were harmed.

Mop, too, obeyed and drank. This time there was no demur from her. Probably she was once again trying methods of ingratiation. We went to bed at nine and I think Mop went to sleep before me. I slept heavily as usual, but I was aware of some disturbance in the night, of having been briefly awakened and spoken to. I remembered this, though not much more for a while, when I finally woke in the morning. It was about seven, a pearly morning of birdsong, and Mop was sitting on the window seat in her nightdress.

She looked awful, as if she had got a bad cold coming or had just been sick.

"I tried to wake you up in the night," she said.

"I thought you had," I said. "Did you have a dream?"

She shook her head. "I woke up and I heard the clock strike one and then I heard footsteps on the path down there."

"In this garden, d'you mean?" I said. "Going or coming?"

"I don't know," she said oddly. "They must have been coming."

"It was a burglar," I said. "We ought to go down and see if things have been stolen."

"It wasn't a burglar." Mop was getting angry with me and her face was blotchy. "I did go down. I lay awake for a bit and I didn't hear any more, but I couldn't go back to sleep and I wanted a drink of water. So I went down."

"Well, go on," I said.

But Mop couldn't go on. And even I, insensitive and unsympathetic to her as I was, could see had been badly frightened, was still frightened, and then I remembered what had wakened me in the night, exactly what had happened. I remembered being brought to brief consciousness by the choking gasps of someone who is screaming in her sleep. Mop had screamed herself awake and the words she had spoken to me had been, "The vinegar mother! The vinegar mother!"

"You had a nightmare," I said.

"Oh, shut up," said Mop. "You never listen. I shan't ever tell you anything again."

But later in the day she did tell me. I think that by this time she had got it into some sort of proportion, although she was still very frightened when she got to the climax of what she insisted couldn't have been a dream. She had, she said, gone downstairs about half an hour after she heard the footsteps in the garden. She hadn't put a light on, as the moon was bright. The dining-room door was partly open, and when she looked inside she saw a hooded figure crouched in a chair by the window. The figure was all in brown, and Mop said she saw the hood slide back and disclose its face. The thing that had made her scream and scream was this face which wasn't a face at all, but a shapeless mass of liver.

"You dreamed it," I said. "You must have. You were in bed when you screamed, so you must have been dreaming."

"I did go down," Mop insisted.

"Maybe you did," I said, "but the other bit was a dream.

Your mother would have come if she'd heard you screaming downstairs."

No more was said about the dream or whatever it was after that, and on Saturday Mr Felton arrived and took us to the Young Farmers' Show at Marks Tey. He brought me my parents' love and the news that my eldest brother had passed his exam and got seven O Levels, and I was happy. He went shooting with Peter Elsworthy on Sunday afternoon, and Peter came back with him and promised to drive me and Mop and Mrs Felton to the seaside for the day on Tuesday.

It was a beautiful day that Tuesday, perhaps the best of all the days at Sanctuary, and I, who, on the morning after Mop's dream, had begun to wonder about making that deceitful phone call from the village, felt I could happily remain till term began. We took a picnic lunch and swam in the wide shallow sea. Mrs Felton wore a proper dress of blue and white cotton which made her brown skin look like a tan, and had smoothed down her hair, and smiled and was gracious and once called Mop dear. Suddenly I liked Peter Elsworthy. I suppose I had one of those infatuations for him that are fused in young girls by a kind smile, one sentence spoken as to a contemporary, one casual touch of the hand. On that sunny beach I was moved towards him by inexplicable feelings, moved into a passion the sight of him had never before inspired, which was to die as quickly as it had been born when the sun had gone, the sea was left behind, and he was once more Mrs Felton's friend in the front seats of the car.

I had followed him about that day like a little dog, and perhaps it was my unconcealed devotion that drove him to leave us at our gate and refuse even to come in and view the progress of the vinegar mother. His excuse was that he had to accompany his mother to an aunt's for dinner. Mrs Felton sulked ferociously after he had gone and we got a supper of runny scrambled eggs and lemon barley water.

On the following night there appeared on our table a bottle of claret. The phone rang while we were eating, and while Mrs

Felton was away answering it I took the daring step of pouring my wine into the vinegar mother.

"I shall tell her," said Mop.

"I don't care," I said. "I can't drink it, nasty, sour, horrible stuff."

"You shouldn't call my father's wine horrible when you're a guest," said Mop, but she didn't tell Mrs Felton. I think she would have poured her own to follow mine except that she was afraid the level in the vessel would rise too much, or was it that by then nothing would have induced her to come within feet of the culture?

I didn't need wine to make me sleep, but if I had taken it I might have slept more heavily. A thin moonlight was in the room when I woke up to see Mop's bed empty. Mop was standing by the door, holding it half open, and she was trembling. It was a bit eerie in there with Mop's long shadow jumping about against the zigzag beams on the wall. But I couldn't hear a sound.

"What's the matter now?" I said.

"There's someone down there."

"How d'you know? Is there a light on?"

"I heard glass," she said.

How can you hear glass? But I knew what she meant and I didn't much like it. I got up and went over to the doorway and looked down the stairs. There was light coming from under the dining-room door, a white glow that could have been from the moon or from the oil lamp they sometimes used. Then I too heard glass, a chatter of glass against glass and a thin trickling sound.

Mop said in a breathy, hysterical voice, "Suppose she goes about in the night to every place where they've got one? She goes about and watches over them and makes it happen. She's down there now doing it. Listen!"

Glass against glass. . . .

"That's crazy," I said. "It's those books you read."

She didn't say anything. We closed the door and lay in our bed with the bedlamp on. The light made it better. We heard the clock strike twelve. I said, "Can we go to sleep now?" And when Mop nodded I put out the light.

The moon had gone away, covered perhaps by clouds. Into the black silence came a curious drawn-out cry. I know now what it was, but no child of eleven could know. I was only aware then that it was no cry of grief or pain or terror, but of triumph, of something at last attained; yet it was at the same time unhuman, utterly outside the bonds of human restraint.

Mop began to scream.

I had the light on and was jumping up and down on my bed, shouting to her to stop, when the door was flung open and Mrs Felton came in, her hair a wild heathery mass, a dressing gown of quilted silk, black-blood colour, wrapped round her and tied at the waist with savagery. Rage and violence were what I expected. But Mrs Felton said nothing. She did what I had never seen her do, had never supposed anything would make her do. She caught Mop in an embrace and hugged her, rocking her back and forth. They were both crying, swaying on the bed and crying. I heard footsteps on the garden path, soft, stealthy, finally fading away.

Mop said nothing at all about it to me the next day. She withdrew into her books and sulks. I believe now that the isolated demonstration of affection she had received from her mother in the night led her to hope more might follow. But Mrs Felton had become weirdly reserved, as if in some sort of long dream. I noticed with giggly embarrassment that she hardly seemed to see Mop hanging about her, looking into her face, trying to get her attention. When Mop gave up at last and took refuge in the garden with Dr James on demons, Mrs Felton lay on the dining-room sofa, smoking and staring at the ceiling. I went in once to fetch my cardigan—for Mrs Potter was taking me to the mediaeval town at Lavenham for the afternoon—and she was still lying there, smiling strangely to herself, her long brown hands playing with her necklace of reddish-brown beads.

She went off for a walk by herself on Friday afternoon and she was gone for hours. It was very hot, too hot to be in a gar-

den with only thin apple-tree shade. I was sitting at the dining-room table, working on a scrapbook of country-house pictures Mrs Potter had got me to make, and Mop was reading,
when the phone rang. Mop answered it, but from the room
where I was, across the passage, I could hear Mr Felton's
hearty bray.

"How's life treating you, my old Mop?"

I heard it all, how he was coming down that night instead
in the morning and would be here by midnight. She might
pass the message on to her mother, but not to worry as he had
his own key. And his kind regards to jolly old Margarine if she
hadn't, by this time, melted away into a little puddle!

Mrs Felton came back at five in Peter Elsworthy's car. There
were leaves in her hair and bits of grass on the back of her
skirt. They pored over the vinegar mother, moving it back into
a cool, dark corner, and enthusing over the colour of the liquor
under the floating liver-like mass.

"A tender plant that mustn't get overheated," said Peter Elsworthy, picking a leaf out of Mrs Felton's hair and laughing. I
wondered why I had ever liked him or thought him kind.

Mop and I were given rosé with our supper out of a dumpy
little bottle with a picture of cloisters on its label. By now Mrs
Felton must have learned that I didn't need wine to make me
sleep, so she didn't insist on my having more than one glass.
The vinegar mother's vessel was three-quarters full.

I was in bed and Mop nearly undressed when I remembered
about her father's message.

"I forgot to tell her," said Mop, yawning and heavy-eyed.

"You could go down and tell her now."

"She'd be cross. Besides, he's got his key."

"You don't like going down in the dark by yourself," I said.
Mop didn't answer. She got into bed and pulled the sheet over
her head.

We never spoke to each other again.

She didn't return to school that term, and at the end of it my
mother told me she wasn't coming back. I never learned what
happened to her. The last—almost the last—I remember of her

was her thin sallow face that lately had always looked bewildered, and the dark circles round her old-woman's eyes. I remember the books on the bedside table: *Fifty Haunted
Houses*, the *Works of Sheridan Lefanu*, *The Best of Montague
Rhodes James*. The pale lacquering of moonlight in that room
with its beams and its slanted ceiling. The silence of night in
an old and haunted countryside. Wine breath in my throat and
wine weariness bringing heavy sleep. . . .

Out of that thick slumber I was awakened by two sharp ex-
plosions and the sound of breaking glass. Mop had gone from
the bedroom before I was out of bed, scarcely aware of where
I was, my head swimming. Somewhere downstairs Mop was
screaming. I went down. The whole house, the house called
Sanctuary, was bright with lights. I opened the dining-room
door.

Mr Felton was leaning against the table, the shotgun still in
his hand. I think he was crying. I don't remember much blood,
only the brown, dead nakedness of Mrs Felton spread on the
floor, with Peter Elsworthy bent over her, holding his
wounded arm. And the smell of gunpowder like fireworks and
the stronger sickening stench of vinegar everywhere, and broken glass in shards, and Mop screaming, plunging a knife again
and again into a thick, slimy liver mass on the carpet.

The Fall of a Coin

The manageress of the hotel took them up two flights of stairs to their room. There was no lift. There was no central heating either and, though April, it was very cold.

"A bit small, isn't it?" said Nina Armadale.

"It's a double room and I'm afraid it's all we had left."

"I suppose I'll have to be thankful it hasn't got a double bed," said Nina.

Her husband winced at that, which pleased her. She went over to the window and looked down into a narrow alley bounded by brick walls. The cathedral clock struck five. Nina imagined what that would be like chiming every hour throughout the night, and maybe every quarter as well, and was glad she had brought her sleeping pills.

The manageress was still making excuses for the lack of accommodation. "You see, there's this big wedding in the cathedral tomorrow. Sir William Tarrant's daughter. There'll be five hundred guests and most of them are putting up in the town."

"We're going to it," said James Armadale. "That's why we're here."

"Then you'll appreciate the problem. Now the bathroom's just down the passage, turn right and it's the third door on the left. Dinner at seven-thirty and breakfast from eight till nine. Oh, and I'd better show Mrs Armadale how to work the gas fire."

"Don't bother," said Nina, enraged. "I can work a gas fire." She was struggling with the wardrobe door, which at first wouldn't open, and when opened refused to close.

The manageress watched her, apparently decided it was hopeless to assist, and said to James, "I really meant about working the gas *meter*. There's a coin-in-the-slot meter—it takes fivepence pieces—and we really find it the best way for guests to manage."

James squatted on the floor beside her and studied the grey metal box. It was an old-fashioned gas meter with brass fittings of the kind he hadn't seen since he had been a student living in a furnished room. A gauge with a red arrow marker indicated the amount of gas paid for, and at present it showed empty. So if you turned the dial on the gas fire to "on" no gas would come from the meter unless you had previously fed it with one or more fivepence pieces. But what was the purpose of that brass handle? There were differences between this contraption and the one he'd had in his college days. Maybe, while his had been for the old toxic coal gas, this had been converted for the supply of natural gas. He looked enquiringly at the manageress, and asked her.

"No, we're still waiting for natural in this part of the country and when it comes the old meters will have to go."

"What's the handle for?"

"You turn it to the left like this, insert your coin in the slot, and then turn it to the right. Have you got fivepence on you?"

James hadn't. Nina had stopped listening, he was glad to see. Perhaps when the inevitable quarrel started, as it would as soon as the woman had gone, it would turn upon the awfulness of going to this wedding, for which he could hardly be blamed, instead of the squalid arrangements in the hotel, for which he could.

"Never mind," the manageress was saying. "You can't go wrong, it's very simple. When you've put your fivepence in, you just turn the handle to the right as far as it will go and you hear the coin fall. Then you can switch on the fire and light the gas. Is that clear?"

James said it was quite clear, thanks very much, and immediately the manageress had left the room. Nina, who wasted no time, said, "Can you tell me one good reason why we couldn't have come here tomorrow?"

"I could tell you several," said James, getting up from the floor, turning his back on that antediluvian thing and the gas fire which looked as if it hadn't given out a therm of heat for about thirty years. "The principal one is that I didn't fancy driving a hundred and fifty miles in a morning coat and top hat."

"Didn't fancy driving with your usual Saturday morning hangover, you mean."

"Let's not start a row, Nina. Let's have a bit of peace for just one evening. Sir William is my company chairman. I have to take it as an honour that we were asked to this wedding, and if we have an uncomfortable evening and night because of it, that can't be helped. It's part of the job."

"Just how pompous can you get?" said Nina with what in a less attractive woman would have been called a snarl. "I wonder what Sir William-Bloody-Tarrant would say if he could see his sales director after he's got a bottle of whisky inside him."

"He doesn't see me," said James, lighting a cigarette, and adding because she hadn't yet broken his spirit, "That's your privilege."

"*Privilege!*" Nina, who had been furiously unpacking her case and throwing clothes on to one of the beds, now stopped doing this because it sapped some of the energy she needed for quarrelling. She sat down on the bed and snapped, "Give me a cigarette. You've no manners, have you? Do you know how uncouth you are? This place'll suit you fine, it's just up to your mark, gas meters and a loo about five hundred yards away. That won't bother you as long as there's a bar. I'll be able to have the *privilege* of sharing my bedroom with a disgusting soak." She drew breath like a swimmer and plunged on. "Do you realise we haven't slept in the same room for two years? Didn't think of that, did you, when you left booking up till the last minute? Or maybe—yes, that was it, my God!—maybe you did think of it. Oh, I know you so well, James Armadale. You thought being in here with me, undressing with me, would work the miracle. I'd come round. I'd—what's the expression?—*resume marital relations.* You got them to give us this—this cell on purpose. You bloody fixed it!"

"No," said James. He said it quietly and rather feebly because he had experienced such a strong inner recoil that he could hardly speak at all.

"You liar! D'you think I've forgotten the fuss you made when I got you to sleep in the spare room? D'you think I've forgotten about that woman, that Frances? I'll never forget and I'll never forgive you. So don't think I'm going to let bygones by bygones when you try pawing me about when the bar closes."

"I shan't do that," said James, reflecting that in a quarter of an hour the bar would be opening. "I shall never again try what you so charmingly describe as pawing you about."

"No, because you know you wouldn't get anywhere. You know you'd get a slap round the face you wouldn't forget in a hurry."

"Nina," he said, "let's stop this. It's hypothetical, it won't happen. If we are going to go on living together—and I suppose we are, though God knows why—can't we try to live in peace?"

She flushed and said in a thick sullen voice, "You should have thought of that before you were unfaithful to me with that woman."

"That," he said, "was three years ago, *three years*. I don't want to provoke you and we've been into this enough times, but you know very well why I was unfaithful to you. I'm only thirty-five, I'm still young. I couldn't stand being permitted *marital relations*—pawing you about, if you like that better— about six times a year. Do I have to go over it all again?"

"Not on my account. It won't make any difference to me what excuses you make." The smoke in the tiny room made her cough and, opening the window, she inhaled the damp, cold air. "You asked me," she said, turning round, "why we have to go on living together. I'll tell you why. Because you married me. I've got a right to you and I'll never divorce you. You've got me till death parts us. Till death, James. Right?"

He didn't answer. An icy blast had come into the room when she had opened the window, and he felt in his pocket. "If you're going to stay in here till dinner," he said, "you'll want the gas fire on. Have you got any fivepence pieces? I haven't, unless I can get some change."

"Oh, you'll get some all right. In the bar. And just for your information, I haven't brought any money with me. That's *your* privilege."

When he had left her alone, she sat in the cold room for some minutes, staring at the brick wall. Till death parts us, she had told him, and she meant it. She would never leave him and he must never be allowed to leave her, but she hoped he would die. It wasn't her fault she was frigid. She had always supposed he understood. She had supposed her good looks and her capacity as housewife and hostess compensated for a revulsion she couldn't help. And it wasn't just against him, but against all men, any man. He had seemed to accept it and to be happy with her. In her sexless way, she had loved him. And then, when he had seemed happier and more at ease than at any time in their marriage, when he had ceased to make those painful demands and had become so sweet to her, so generous with presents, he had suddenly and without shame confessed it. She wouldn't mind, he had told her, he knew that. She wouldn't resent his finding elsewhere what she so evidently disliked giving him. While he provided for her and spent nearly all his leisure with her and respected her as his wife, she should be relieved, disliking sex as she did, that he had found someone else.

He had said it was the pent-up energy caused by her repressions that made her fly at him, beat at him with her hands, scream at him words he didn't know she knew. To her dying day she would remember his astonishment. He had genuinely thought she wouldn't mind. And it had taken weeks of nagging and screaming and threats to make him agree to give Frances up. She had driven him out of her bedroom and settled into the bitter, unremitting vendetta she would keep up till death parted them. Even now, he didn't understand how agonisingly he had hurt her. But there were no more women and he had begun to drink. He was drinking now, she thought, and by nine o'clock he would be stretched out, dead drunk on that bed separated by only eighteen inches from her own.

The room was too cold to sit in any longer. She tried the gas fire, turning on the switch to "full," but the match she held to it refused to ignite it, and presently she made her way downstairs and into a little lounge where there was a coal fire and people were watching television.

They met again at the dinner table.

James Armadale had drunk getting on for half a pint of whisky, and now, to go with the brown Windsor soup and hotted-up roast lamb, he ordered a bottle of burgundy.

"Just as a matter of idle curiosity," said Nina, "why do you drink so much?"

"To drown my sorrows," said James. "The classic reason. Happens to be true in my case. Would you like some wine?"

"I'd better have a glass, hadn't I, otherwise you'll drink the whole bottle."

The dining room was full and most of the other diners were middle-aged or elderly. Many of them, he supposed, would be wedding guests like themselves. He could see that their arrival had been noted and that at the surrounding tables their appearance was being favourably commented upon. It afforded him a thin, wry amusement to think that they would be judged a handsome, well-suited and perhaps happy couple.

"Nina," he said, "we can't go on like this. It's not fair on either of us. We're destroying ourselves and each other. We have to talk about what we're going to do."

"Pick your moments, don't you? I'm not going to talk about it in a public place."

She had spoken in a low, subdued voice, quite different from her hectoring tone in their bedroom, and she shot quick, nervous glances at the neighbouring tables.

"It's because this is a public place that I think we stand a better chance of talking about it reasonably. When we're alone you get hysterical and then neither of us can be rational. If we talk about it now, I think I know you well enough to say you won't scream at me."

"I could walk out though, couldn't I? Besides, you're drunk."

"I am not drunk. Frankly, I probably shall be in an hour's time and that's another reason why we ought to talk here and now. Look, Nina, you don't love me, you've said so often enough, and whatever crazy ideas you have about my having designs on you, I don't love you either. We've been into the reasons for that so many times that I don't need to go into them now, but can't we come to some sort of amicable arrangement to split up?"

"So that you can have all the women you want? So that you can bring that bitch into my house?"

"No," he said, "you can have the house. The court would probably award you a third of my income, but I'll give you more if you want. I'd give you half." He had nearly added, "to be rid of you," but he bit off the words as being too provocative. His speech was already thickening and slurring.

It was disconcerting—though this was what he had wanted —to hear how inhibition made her voice soft and kept her face controlled. The words she used were the same, though. He had heard them a thousand times before. "If you leave me, I'll follow you. I'll go to your office and tell them all about it. I'll sit on your doorstep. I won't be abandoned. I'd rather die. I won't be a divorced woman just because you've got tired of me."

"If you go on like this," he said thickly, "you'll find yourself a widow. Will you like that?"

Had they been alone, she would have screamed the affirmative at him. Because they weren't, she gave him a thin, sharp, and concentrated smile, a smile which an observer might have taken for amusement at some married couple's private joke. "Yes," she said, "I'd like to be a widow, *your* widow. Drink yourself to death, why don't you? That's what you have to do if you want to be rid of me."

The waitress came to their table. James ordered a double brandy and "coffee for my wife." He knew he would never be rid of her. He wasn't the sort of man who can stand public disruption of his life, scenes at work, molestation, the involvement of friends and employers. It must be, he knew, an amicable split or none at all. And since she would never see reason, never understand or forgive, he must soldier on. With the help of this, he thought, as the brandy spread its dim, cloudy euphoria through his brain. He drained his glass quickly, muttered an "excuse me" to her for the benefit of listeners, and left the dining room.

Nina returned to the television lounge. There was a play on whose theme was a marital situation that almost paralleled her own. The old ladies with their knitting and the old men with their after-dinner cigars watched it apathetically. She thought she might take the car and go somewhere for a drive. It didn't much matter where, anywhere would do that was far enough from this hotel and James and that cathedral clock whose chimes split the hours into fifteen-minute segments with long brazen peals. There must be somewhere in this town where one could get a decent cup of coffee, some cinema maybe where they weren't showing a film about marriage or what people, she thought shudderingly, called sexual relationships. She went upstairs to get the car keys and some money.

James was fast asleep. He had taken off his tie and his shoes, but otherwise he was fully dressed, lying on his back and snoring. Stupid of him not to get under the covers. He'd freeze. Maybe he'd die of exposure. Well, she wasn't going to cover him up, but she'd close the window for when she came in. The car keys were in his jacket pocket, mixed up with a lot of loose change. The feel of his warm body through the material made her shiver. His breath smelt of spirits and he was sweating in spite of the cold. Among the change were two fivepence pieces. She'd take one of those and keep it till the morning to feed that gas meter. It would be horrible dressing for that wedding in here at zero temperature. Why not feed it now so that it would be ready for the morning, ready to turn the gas fire on and give her some heat when she came in at midnight, come to that?

The room was faintly illuminated by the yellow light from the street lamp in the alley. She crouched down in front of the gas fire, and noticed she hadn't turned the dial to "off" after her match had failed to ignite the jets. It wouldn't do to feed that meter now with the dial turned to "full" and have fivepence worth of old-fashioned toxic gas flood the room. Not with the window tight shut and not a crack round that heavy old door. Slowly she put her hand out to turn off the dial.

Her fingers touched it. Her hand remained still, poised. She heard her heart begin to thud softly in the silence as the idea in all its brilliant awfulness took hold of her. Wouldn't do . . . ? Was she mad? It wouldn't do to feed that meter now with the gas-fire dial turned to "full"? What would do as well, as efficiently, as finally? She withdrew her hand and clasped it in the other to steady it.

Rising to her feet, she contemplated her sleeping husband. The sweat was standing on his pale forehead now. He snored as rhythmically, as stertorously, as her own heart beat. A widow, she thought, alone and free in her own unshared house. Not divorced, despised, disowned, laughed at by judges and solicitors for her crippling frigidity, not mocked by that Frances and her successors, but a widow whom all the world would pity and respect. Comfortably-off too, if not rich, with an income from James's life assurance and very likely a pension from Sir William Tarrant.

James wouldn't wake up till midnight. No, that was wrong. He wouldn't *have* wakened up till midnight. What she meant was he wouldn't wake up at all.

The dial on the gas fire was still on, full on. She took the fivepence coin and tiptoed over to the meter. Nothing would wake him but still she tiptoed. The window was tight shut, with nothing beyond it but that alley, that glistening lamp, and the towering wall of the cathedral.

She studied the meter, kneeling down. It was the first time in her sheltered, cosseted, snug life that she had ever actually seen a coin-in-the-slot gas meter. But if morons like hotel servants and the sort of people who would stay in a place like this could work it, she could. There was the slot where the coin went in, there the gauge whose red arrow showed empty. All you had to do, presumably, was slip in the coin, fiddle about with that handle, and then, if the gas-fire dial was on, toxic coal gas—the kind of gas that had killed thousands in the past, careless old people, suicides, accident-prone fools—would rapidly begin to seep out of the unlighted jets in the fire. James wouldn't smell it. Drink paralysed him into an unconsciousness as deep as that which her own sleeping tablets brought to her.

Nina was certain it wouldn't matter that she hadn't attended closely to the manageress's instructions. What had she said? Turn the handle to the left, insert the coin, turn it to the right. She hesitated for a moment, just long enough for brief fractured memories to cross her mind—James when they were first married, James patient and self-denying on their honeymoon, James promising that her coldness didn't matter, that with time and love . . . James confessing with a defiant smirk, throwing Frances's name at her, James going on a three-day bender because she couldn't pretend the wound he'd given her was just a surface scratch, James drunk night after night after night. . . .

She didn't hesitate for long.

She got her coat, put the car keys in her handbag. Then she knelt down again between the gas fire and the meter. First she checked that the dial, which was small and almost at ground level, was set at "full." She took hold of the brass handle on the meter and turned it to the left. The coin slot was now fully exposed and open. She pressed in the fivepence piece and flicked the handle to the right. There was no need to wait for the warning smell, oniony, acrid, of the escaping gas. Without looking back, she walked swiftly from the room, closing the door behind her.

The cathedral clock chimed the last quarter before nine.

When the bar closed at eleven-thirty, the crowd of people coming upstairs and chattering in loud voices would have awakened even the deepest sleeper. They woke James. He didn't move for some time but lay there with his eyes open till he heard the clock chime midnight. When the last stroke died away he reached out and turn on the bedside lamp. The light was like knives going into his head, and he groaned. But he felt like this most nights at midnight and there was no use making a fuss. Who would hear or care if he did? Nina was evidently still downstairs in that lounge. It was too much to hope she might stay there all night out of fear of being alone with him. No, she'd be up now the television had closed down and she'd start berating him for his drunkenness and his infidelity—not that there had been any since Frances—and they would lie there bickering and smarting until grey light mingled with that yellow light, and the cathedral clock told them it was dawn.

And yet she had been so sweet once, so pathetic and desperate in her sad failure. It had never occurred to him to blame her, though his body suffered. And his own solution, honestly confessed, might have worked so well for all three of them if she had been rational. He wondered vaguely, for the thousandth time, why he had been such a fool as to confess, when, with a little deception, he might be happier now than at any time in his marriage. But he was in no fit state to think. Where had that woman said the bathroom was? Turn right down the passage and the third door on the left. He lay there till the clock struck the quarter before he felt he couldn't last out any longer and he'd have to find it.

The cold air in the passage—God, it was more like January than April—steadied him a little and made his head bang and throb. He must be crazy to go on like this. What the hell was he doing, turning himself into an alcoholic at thirty-five? Because there were no two ways about it, he was an alcoholic all right, a drunk. And if he stayed with Nina he'd be a dead alcoholic by forty. But how can you leave a woman who won't leave you? Give up his job, run away, go to the ends of the earth. . . . It wasn't unusual for him to have wild thoughts like this at midnight, but when the morning came he knew he would just soldier on.

He stayed in the bathroom for about ten minutes. Coming back along the passage, he heard footsteps on the stairs, and knowing he must look horrible and smell horribly of liquor, he retreated behind the open door of what proved to be a broom cupboard. But it was only his wife. She approached their room door slowly as if she were bracing herself to face something—

himself, probably, he thought. Had she really that much loathing of him that she had to draw in her breath and clench her
hands before confronting him? She was very pale. She looked
ill and frightened, and when she had opened the door and
gone inside he heard her give a kind of shrill gasp that was almost a shriek.

He followed her into the room, and when she turned and
saw him he thought she was going to faint. She had been pale
before, but now she turned paper white. Once, when he had
still loved her and had hoped he might teach her to love him,
he would have been concerned. But now he didn't care, and all
he said was, "Been watching something nasty on the T.V.?"

She didn't answer him. She sat down on her bed and put her
head into her hands. James undressed and got into bed. Presently Nina got up and began taking her clothes off slowly and
mechanically. His head and body had begun to twitch as they
did when he was recovering from the effects of a drinking
bout. It left him wide awake. He wouldn't sleep again for
hours. He watched her curiously but dispassionately, for he
had long ago ceased to derive the slightest pleasure or excitement from seeing her undress. What intrigued him now was
that, though she was evidently in some sort of state of shock,
her hands shaking, she still couldn't discard those modest sub-
terfuges of hers, her way of turning her back when she stepped
out of her dress, of pulling her nightgown over her head before
she took off her underclothes.

She put on her dressing gown and went to the bathroom.
When she came back her face was greasy where she had
cleaned off the make-up and she was shivering.

"You'd better take a sleeping tablet," he said.

"I've already taken one in the bathroom. I wanted a bath
but there wasn't any hot water." Getting into bed, she ex-
claimed in her normal fierce way, "Nothing works in this
damned place! Nothing goes right!"

"Put out the light and go to sleep. Anyone would think you'd
got to spend the rest of your life here instead of just one
night."

She made no reply. They never said good night to each other. When she had put her light out the room wasn't really dark because a street lamp was still lit in the alley outside. He had seldom felt less like sleep, and now he was aware of a sensation he hadn't expected because he hadn't thought about it. He didn't want to share a bedroom with her.

That cold modesty, which had once been enticing, now repelled him. He raised himself on one elbow and peered at her. She lay in the defensive attitude of a woman who fears assault, flat on her stomach, her arms folded under her head. Although the sleeping pill had taken effect and she was deeply asleep, her body seemed stiff, prepared to galvanise into violence at a touch. She smelt cold. A sour saltiness emanated from her as if there were sea water in her veins instead of blood. He thought of real women with warm blood, women who awoke from sleep when their husband's faces neared theirs, who never recoiled but smiled and put out their arms. For ever she would keep him from them until the drink or time made him as frozen as she.

Suddenly he knew he couldn't stay in that room. He might do something dreadful, beat her up perhaps or even kill her. And much as he wanted to be rid of her, spend no more time with her, no more money on her, the notion of killing her was as absurd as it was grotesque. It was unthinkable. But he couldn't stay here.

He got up and put on his dressing gown. He'd go to that lounge where she'd watched television, take a blanket, and spend the rest of the night there. She wouldn't wake till nine and by then he'd be back, ready to dress for that wedding. Funny, really, their going to a wedding, to watch someone else getting into the same boat. But it wouldn't be the same boat, for if office gossip was to be relied on, Sir William's daughter had already opened her warm arms to many men. . . .

The cathedral clock struck one. By nine the room would be icy and they'd need that gas fire. Why not put a fivepence piece in the meter now so that the fire would work when he wanted it?

The fire itself lay in shadow but the meter was clearly illuminated by the street lamp. James knelt down, trying to remember the instructions of the manageress. Better try it out first before he put his coin in, his only fivepence coin. Strange, that. He could have sworn he'd had two when he first went to bed.

What had that woman said? Turn the handle to the left, insert the coin, turn the handle to the right. . . . No, turn it to the right as far as it will go until *you hear the coin fall.* Keeping hold of his coin—he didn't want to waste it if what Nina said was true and nothing worked in this place—he turned the handle to the left, then hard to the right as far as it would go.

Inside the meter a coin fell with a small dull clang. The red arrow marker on the gauge, which had stood at empty, moved along to register payment. Good. He was glad he hadn't wasted his money. The previous guest must have put a coin in and failed to turn the handle until it fell. So Nina had been wrong about things not working. Still, it wasn't unusual for her to get the wrong idea, not unusual at all. . . .

Gas would come through now once the dial was switched on. James checked that the window was shut to keep out the cold, gave a last look at the sleeping, heavily sedated woman, and went out of the room, closing the door behind him.

Almost Human

The Chief was stretched out on the settee, half asleep. Monty sat opposite him, bolt upright in his chair. Neither of them moved as Dick helped himself to gin and water. They didn't care for strong drink, the Chief not even for the smell of it, though it wasn't his way to show his feelings. Monty would sometimes drink beer in the George Tavern with Dick. It was cigarette smoke that upset him, and now as he caught a whiff from Dick's Capstan, he sneezed.

"Bless you," said Dick.

Better smoke the rest of it in the kitchen while he was getting their supper. It wasn't fair on Monty to start him coughing at his age, bring on his bronchitis maybe. There was nothing Dick wouldn't have done for Monty's comfort, but when he had taken the steak out of the fridge and gone once more into the sitting room for his drink, it was the Chief he addressed. Monty was his friend and the best company in the world. You couldn't look on the Chief in that light, but more as a boss to be respected and deferred to.

"Hungry, Chief?" he said.

The Chief got off the settee and walked into the kitchen. Dick went after him. It was almost dark outside now but enough light remained to show Dick Monty's coat, the old check one, still hanging on the clothesline. Better take it in in case it rained in the night. Dick went out into the yard, hoping against hope old Tom, his next-door neighbour, wouldn't see the kitchen light and come out. Such hope was always vain. He'd got the first of the pegs out when he heard the door open and the cracked, whining voice.

"Going to be a cold night."

"Mmm," said Dick.

"Shouldn't be surprised if there was to be a frost."

Who cared? Dick saw the great angular shadow of the Chief appear in the rectangle of light. Good, that would fix him. Standing erect, as he now was against the fence, the Chief was a good head taller than old Tom, who backed away, grinning nervously.

"Come on, Chief," said Dick. "Suppertime."

"Just like children, aren't they?" old Tom whined. "Almost human, it's uncanny. Look at him. He understands every word you say."

Dick didn't answer. He followed the Chief into the kitchen and slammed the door. Nothing angered him more than the way people thought they were paying compliments to animals by comparing them with people. As if the Chief and Monty weren't in every way, mentally, physically, morally, a hundred times better than any human being he'd ever known. Just like children—what a load of crap. Children wanting their supper would be crying, making a nuisance of themselves, getting under his feet. His dogs, patient, stoical, single-minded, sat still and silent, watching while he filled the earthenware bowls with steak and meal and vitamin supplement. And when the bowls were placed side by side on the floor, they moved towards them with placid dignity.

Dick watched them feed. Monty's appetite, at fourteen, was as good as ever, though he took longer about it than the Chief. His teeth weren't what they had been. When the old dog had cleared his plate he did what he'd always done ever since he was a pup, came over to Dick and laid his grey muzzle in the palm of the outstretched hand. Dick fondled his ears.

"Good old dog," Dick said. He scorned the popular way of calling dogs boy. They weren't boys. Boys were dirty and smelly and noisy and uncontrolled. "You're a cracker, you are. You're a fine old dog."

The Chief behaved in a grander manner. Such signs of affection and gratitude would have been inconsistent with his pedigree and his dignified presence. Dick and Monty knew their place and they both stepped aside to allow the Chief to pass majestically through the doorway and resume his position on the settee. Dick pushed Monty's chair nearer to the radiator. Half past six. He finished his gin.

"I have to go out now," he said, "but I'll be back by ten at the latest, so you get a bit of shut-eye and when I come back we'll all have a good walk. O.K.?"

Monty came to the front door with him. He always had and always would, though his hind legs were stiff with rheumatism. We all have to get old, Dick thought; I'll have to face up to it, I'm going to lose him this year or next. . . . He knelt down by the door and did what he'd never done to man, woman, or child—performed that disgusting act which sickened him when he saw it done by human beings to human beings. Holding Monty's head in his hands, he pressed his lips to the wrinkled forehead. Monty wagged his tail and emitted little grunts of happiness. Dick closed the door and got his car out of the garage.

He drove it two or three hundred yards down the street to the phone box. For business he never used his own phone but one or other of the call boxes between his house and the George Tavern. Five minutes to go and the bell inside it would begin to ring. Unless something went wrong again, of course. Unless, once more, things weren't working out the way she'd planned them. The stupid—what? Dick hated the habit of using the names of female animals—bitch, cow, mare—as insulting epithets for women. When he wanted to express his loathing for the sex he chose one of the succinct four-letter words or the five-letter one that was the worst he could think of—woman. He used it now, rolling it on his tongue. Stupid, bloody, greedy, God-damned *woman!*

When his watch showed nearly a quarter to seven, he went into the box. He only had to wait sixty seconds. The bell began to ring on the dot of a quarter to. Dick lifted the receiver and spoke the password that would tell her it was he and not some interfering busybody answering phones for the hell of it.

He'd never heard her voice before. It was nervous, upperclass, a thousand miles from any world in which he'd ever moved. "It's going to be all right tonight," she said.

"About time." All their previous transactions had been arranged through his contact and every plan had come to grief through a hold-up at her end. It was six weeks since he'd had the tip-off and the first instalment. "Let's have it then."

She cleared her throat. "Listen, I don't want you to know anything about us—who we are, I mean. Agreed?"

As if he cared who they were or what dirty passions had brought her to this telephone, this conspiracy. But he said contemptuously, "It'll be in the papers, won't it?"

Fear thinned her voice. "You could blackmail me!"

"And you could blackmail me, come to that. It's a risk we have to take. Now get on with it, will you?"

"All right. He's not been well but he's better now and he's started taking his usual walk again. He'll leave this house at half past eight and walk through the West Heath path towards the Finchley Road. You don't have to know why or where he's going. That's not your business."

"I couldn't care less," said Dick.

"It'll be best for you to wait in one of the lonelier bits of the path, as far from the houses as you can."

"You can leave all that to me. I know the area. How'll I know it's him?"

"He's fifty, well-built, middle height, silver hair, small moustache. He won't be wearing a hat. He'll have on a black overcoat with a black fur collar over a grey tweed suit. He ought to get to the middle of the West Heath path by ten to nine." The voice wavered slightly. "It won't be too messy, will it? How will you do it?"

"D'you expect me to tell you that on the phone?"

"No, perhaps not. You've had the first thousand?"

"For six weeks," said Dick.

"I couldn't help the delay. It wasn't my fault. You'll get the rest within a week, in the way you got the first. . . ."

"Through the usual channel. Is that all? Is that all I have to know?"

"I think so," she said. "There's one other thing—no, it doesn't matter." She hesitated. "You won't fail me, will you? Tonight's the last chance. If it doesn't happen tonight, there's no point in its happening at all. The whole situation changes tomorrow and I shan't . . ."

"Good-bye," said Dick, slamming down the receiver to cut short the voice that was growing hysterical. He didn't want to know any of the circumstances or be involved in her sick emotions. Bloody—*woman*. Not that he had any qualms. He'd have killed a hundred men for what she was paying him to kill one, and he was interested only in the money. What did it matter to him who he was or she was or why she wanted him out of the way? She might be his wife or his mistress. So what? Such relationships were alien to Dick and the thought of what they implied nauseated him, kissing, embracing, the filthy act they did like—no, not like animals; animals were decent, decorous—like people. He spat into the corner of the kiosk and came out into the cold evening air.

As he drove up towards Hampstead, he thought of the money. It would be just enough to bring his accumulated savings to his target. For years, ever since he'd got Monty from the pet shop, he'd been working to this end. Confidence tricks, a couple of revenge killings, the odd beating up, casing places for robbery, they'd all been lucrative, and by living modestly—the dogs' food was his biggest expense—he'd got nearly enough to buy the house he'd got his eye on. It was to be in Scotland, on the north-west coast and miles from a village, a granite croft with enough grounds round it for Monty and the Chief to run free all day. He liked to think of the way they'd look when they saw their own bit of moorland, their own rabbits to chase. He'd have sufficient left over to live on without working for the rest of his life, and maybe he'd get more animals, a horse perhaps, a couple of goats. But no more dogs while Monty was alive. That wouldn't be fair, and it seemed wrong, the height of treachery, to make plans for after Monty was dead. . . .

What there wouldn't be anywhere in the vicinity of his house were people. With luck he wouldn't hear a human voice from one month's end to another. The human race, its ugly face, would be excluded for ever. In those hills with Monty and Chief he'd forget how for forty years they'd pressed around him with their cruelty and their baseness, his drunken, savage father, his mother who'd cared only for men and having a good time. Then, later, the foster home, the reform school, the factory girls sniggering at his shyness and his pimply face, the employers who wouldn't take him because he had a record instead of an education. At last he'd have peace.

So he had to kill a man to get it? It wouldn't be the first time. He would kill him without passion or interest, as easily as the slaughterer kills the lamb and with as little mercy. A light blow to the head first, just enough to stun him—Dick wasn't worried about giving pain but about getting blood on his clothes—and then that decisive pressure just here, on the hyoid. . . .

Fingering his own neck to site the spot, Dick parked the car and went into a pub for another small gin and water and a sandwich. The licensee's cat came and sat on his knee. Animals were drawn to him as by a magnet. They knew who their friends were. Pity really that the Chief had such a hatred of cats, otherwise he might have thought of adding a couple to his Scottish menagerie. Half past seven. Dick always allowed himself plenty of time to do a job, take it slowly, that was the way. He put the cat gently on the floor.

By eight he'd driven up through Hampstead village, along Branch Hill by the Whitestone Pond, and parked the car in West Heath Road. A fine starry night, frosty too, like that old fool had said it would be. For a few minutes he sat in the car, turning over in his mind whether there was anything at all to connect him with the woman he'd spoken to. No, there was nothing. His contact was as reliable and trustworthy as any human being could be and the method of handing over the money was foolproof. As for associating him with the man he was going to kill—Dick knew well that the only safe murder is the murder of a complete stranger. Fortunately for him and his clients, he was a stranger to the whole world of men.

Better go up and look at the path now. He put the car in Templewood Avenue as near as he could to the point where the path left it to wind across West Heath. This was to be on the safe side. There weren't any real risks, but it was always as well to ensure a quick getaway. He strolled into the path. It led between the fences of gardens, a steep lane about five feet wide, with steps here and there where the incline grew too sharp. At the summit was a street lamp and another about fifty yards further on where the path became walled. Between the lights was a broader sandy space, dotted about with trees and shrubs. He'd do it here, Dick decided. He'd stand among the trees until the man appeared from the walled end, wait until he left the first pool of light but hadn't yet reached the second, and catch him in the darkest part. No roofs were visible, only the backs of vast gardens, jungly and black, and though the stars were bright, the moon was a thin white curve that gave little light.

Luckily, the bitter cold was keeping most people indoors. As soon as this thought had passed through his mind, he heard footsteps in the distance and his hand tightened on the padded metal bar in his pocket. But not yet, surely? Not at twenty-five past eight? Or had that fool woman made another of her mistakes? No, this was a girl. The click of her heels told him that, and then he saw her emerge into the lamplight. With a kind of sick curiosity he watched her approach, a tall, slim girl yet with those nauseating repulsive bulges under her coat. She walked swiftly and nervously in this lonely place, looking with swift, birdlike glances to the right and the left, her whole body deformed by the tight, stupid clothes she wore and the stiff stance her heels gave her. No animal grace, no assurance. Dick would dearly have loved to give her a scare, jump on her and shake her till her teeth chattered, or chase her down those steps. But the idea of unnecessary contact with human flesh repelled him. Besides, she'd see his face and know him again when they found the body and raised the hue and cry. What would happen to Monty and the Chief if they caught him and put him inside? The thought made him shudder.

He let the girl pass by and settled down to wait again. A thin wrack of cloud passed across the stars. All to the good if it got a bit darker. . . . Twenty to nine. He'd have left by now and be coming up to the Whitestone Pond.

Dick would have liked a cigarette but decided it wasn't worth the risk. The smell might linger and alert the man. Again he fingered the metal bar and the thin coil of picture cord. In a quarter of an hour, with luck, it would all be over. Then back home to the Chief and Monty for their evening walk, and tomorrow he'd get on to that house agent he'd seen advertising in the Sunday paper. Completely isolated, he'd say. It must be completely isolated and with plenty of land, maybe near the sea. The Chief would enjoy a swim, though he'd probably never had one in his life, spent as it had been in the dirty back streets of a city. But all dogs could swim by the light of nature. Different from human beings, who had to be taught like they had to be taught every damn-fool stupid thing they undertook. . . .

Footsteps. Yes, it was time. Ten to nine, and evidently he was of a punctual habit. So much the worse for him. Dick kept perfectly still, staring at the dark hole between the walls, until the vague shape of his quarry appeared at the end of the tunnel. As the man came towards the light, he tensed, closing his hand over the bar. Her description had been precise. It was a stoutish figure that the lamplight showed him, its gleam falling on thick silver hair and the glossy black fur of a coat collar. If Dick had ever felt the slightest doubt as to the ethics of what he was about to do, that sight would have dispelled it. Did scum like that ever pause to think of the sufferings of trapped animals, left to die in agony just to have their pelts stuck on some rich bastard's coat? Dick gathered saliva in his mouth and spat silently but viciously into the undergrowth.

The man advanced casually and confidently and the dark space received him. Dick stepped out from among the trees, raised his arm and struck. The man gave a grunt, not much louder than a hiccup, and fell heavily. There was no blood, not a spot. Bracing himself to withstand the disgust contact with a warm, heavily fleshed body would bring, Dick thrust his arms under the sagging shoulders and dragged him under the lamp.

He was unconscious and would be for five minutes—except that in five minutes or less he'd be dead.

Dick didn't waste time examining the face. He had no interest in it. He put his cosh back in his pocket and brought out the cord. A slip knot here, slide it round here, then a quick tightening of pressure on the hyoid . . .

A soft sound stayed him, the cord still slack in his hands. It wasn't a footstep he'd heard but a light padding. He turned sharply. Out of the tunnel, tail erect, nose to ground, came a hound dog, a black and tan and white basset. It was one of the handsomest dogs Dick had ever seen, but he didn't want to see it now. Christ, he thought, it'd be bound to come up to him. They always did.

And sure enough the hound hesitated as it left the darkness and entered the patch of light where Dick was. It lifted its head and advanced on him, waving its tail. Dick cursed fate, not the dog, and held out his hand.

"Good dog," he whispered. "You're a cracker. You're a fine dog, you are. But get out of it now, go off home."

The hound resisted his hand with an aloof politeness and, by-passing him, thrust its nose against the unconscious man's face. Dick didn't like that much. The guy might wake up.

"Come on now," he said, laying his hands firmly on the glossy tricolour coat. "This is no place for you. You get on with your hunting or whatever."

But the basset wouldn't go. Its tail trembled and it whined. It looked at Dick and back at the man and began to make those soft hound cries that are halfway between a whimper and a whistle. And then Dick loosened his hold on the thick, warm pelt. A terrible feeling had come over him, dread coupled with nausea. He felt in the pocket of the black fur-collared coat and brought out what he was afraid to find there —a plaited leather dog leash.

That God-damned woman! Was that what she'd meant about one other thing but it didn't matter? That this guy would be coming along here because he was taking his dog for a walk? Didn't matter—Christ! It didn't matter the poor little devil seeing its owner murdered and then having to make its own way home across one of the busiest main roads out of London. Or maybe she'd thought he'd kill the dog too. The sheer inhumanity of it made his blood boil. He wanted to kick the man's face as he lay there, but didn't like to, couldn't somehow, with the dog looking on.

He wouldn't be done, though. His house in Scotland was waiting for him. He owed it to the Chief and Monty to get that house. All that money wasn't going to be given up just because she'd gone and got things wrong again. There were ways. Like putting the dog on the leash and taking him back across the road by the Whitestone Pond. He'd be safe then. And so by that time, thought Dick, would his owner who was already stirring and moaning. Or he could put him in the car. God knew, he was gentle enough, utterly trusting, not suspecting what Dick had done, was going to do. . . . And then? Kill the man and take the dead man's dog home? Be seen with the dog in his car? That was a laugh. Tie him up to a lamppost? He'd never in his life tied up a dog and he wasn't going to start now.

A cold despair took hold of him. He bore the dog no malice, felt for him no anger, nothing more than the helpless resignation of a father whose child has come into a room and interrupted his love-making. The child comes first—inevitably.

Slowly he put away the cord. He lifted the silver head roughly and the man groaned. There had been a hard metal object in the pocket where the leash was, a brandy flask. Dick uncapped it and poured some of the liquid down the man's throat. The hound watched, thumping its tail.

"Where—where am I? Wha—what happened?"

Dick didn't bother to answer him.

"I had a—a bang on the head. God, my head's sore. I was mugged, was I?" He felt in his pocket and scrabbled with a wallet. "Not touched, thank God. I'll—I'll try to sit up. God, that's better. Where's Bruce? Oh, there he is. Good boy, Bruce. I'm glad he's all right."

"He's a fine dog," Dick said remotely, and then, "Come on, you'd better hang on to me. I've got a car."

"You're most kind, most kind. What a blessing for me you came along when you did."

Dick said nothing. He almost heaved when the man clung to his arm and leant on him. Bruce anchored to his leash, they set off down the steps to the car. It was a relief to be free of that touch, that solid weight that smelt of the sweat of terror. Dick got Bruce on to the back seat and stroked him, murmuring reassuring words.

The house he was directed to was a big one, almost a mansion on the East Heath. Lights blazed in its windows. Dick hauled the man out and propelled him up to the front door, leaving Bruce to follow. He rang the bell and a uniformed maid answered. Behind her, in the hall, stood a tall young woman in evening dress.

She spoke the one word "Father!" and her voice was sick with dismay. But it was the same voice. He recognised it just as she recognised his when, turning away from the glimpse of wealth in that hall, he said, "I'll be off now."

Their eyes met. Her face was chalk-white, made distorted and ugly by the destruction of her hopes. She let her father take her arm and then she snapped, "What happened?"

"I was mugged, dear, but I'm all right now. This gentleman happened to come along at the opportune moment. I haven't thanked him properly yet." He put out his hand to Dick. "You must come in. You must let us have your name. No, I insist. You probably saved my life. I could have died of exposure out there."

"Not you," said Dick. "Not with that dog of yours."

"A lot of use he was! Not much of a bodyguard, are you, Bruce?"

Dick bent down and patted the dog. He shook off the detaining hand and said as he turned away, "You'll never know how much use he was."

He got into the car without looking back. In the mirror, as he drove away, he saw the woman retreat into the house while her father stood dizzily on the path, making absurd gestures of gratitude after his rescuer.

Dick got home by a quarter to ten. Monty was waiting for him in the hall, but the Chief was still in the sitting room on the settee. Dick put on their leashes and his best coat on Monty and opened the front door.

"Time for a beer before the pub closes, Mont," he said, "and then we'll go on the common." He and the dogs sniffed the diesel-laden air and Monty sneezed. "Bless you," said Dick. "Lousy hole, this, isn't it? It's a bloody shame but you're going to have to wait a bit longer for our place in Scotland."

Slowly, because Monty couldn't make it fast any more, the three of them walked up towards the George Tavern.

Divided We Stand

It was Mother who told Marjorie about Pauline's friend, not Pauline herself. Pauline never said much. She had always been a sulky girl, though hardly a girl any more, Marjorie thought. Mother waited until she had gone out of the room to get the tea and then, leaning forward in her chair, whispering, closing both her hands over the top of her walking stick, she said, "Pauline's got a gentleman friend."

"How do you know?" asked Marjorie—a stupid question, as there was only one way Mother could know, seeing that she and Pauline were always together.

"He was here last night. He came after I'd gone to bed but I could hear them talking down here. He didn't stay long and when he was going I heard him say, 'Speaking as a doctor, Pauline . . .' so I reckon she met him when she was in *that place.*"

Marjorie didn't like to hear "that place" spoken of. It was foolish—narrow-minded, George said—but a lunatic asylum is a lunatic asylum even if they do call them mental hospitals these days, and she didn't care to think of her sister having been in one. A mental breakdown—why couldn't the specialist have called it a *nervous* breakdown?—was such an awful thing to have in the family.

"Maybe he came—well, professionally," she said. "Didn't you ask her?"

"I didn't like to, dear. You know what Pauline is."

Marjorie did. And now they had to stop talking about it, for Pauline had come in with the tea things. She buttered a scone for Mother, cut it into small pieces, tucked a napkin round Mother's neck, and all this she did in silence.

"Why are you using the best china?" Mother said.

"What d'you mean, dear?" said Marjorie. "This is the old blue china you always use."

"No, it isn't."

Marjorie started once more to protest, but Pauline interrupted her. "Leave it. She can't see. You know how bad her

sight is." She gave Mother one of her bright nurse's smiles.
"O.K., so we're using the best china," she said, and she wiped
the corners of Mother's mouth with a tissue.

Not long after they had finished, Marjorie left. She had the
perfectly valid excuse of George and the children. It wasn't
possible for her to stay long—Mother understood that. And she
had, after all, washed the dishes before she went, with Pauline's eye on her and Pauline's silence more difficult to bear
than any noise. On Saturday afternoon she was back again,
"just looking in" as she put it, on her way to the shops.

"He was here again last night," Mother whispered.

"Who was?"

"That doctor friend of Pauline's. He was here ever so late. I
rang my bell for Pauline because I wanted to go to the toilet.
It was gone eleven and I could hear him talking after I'd gone
back to bed."

Pauline had been in the garden, getting the clean linen,
drawsheets and towels and napkins and Mother's nightgowns,
in from the line. When she re-entered the room Marjorie studied her appearance uneasily. Her sister looked exhausted. She
was a tall, gaunt woman, dark and swarthy, and now she was
so thin that the shapeless old trousers she wore hung loose
against her hips. Dark shadows ringed her eyes, and those eyes
had a glazed look, due perhaps to the drugs she had been on
ever since she came out of "that place."

"Have I got a spot?" said Pauline. "Or am I so lovely you
can't take your eyes off me?"

"Sorry, I was off in a dream." Marjorie said she had better
get away before the shops shut, and Mother thanked her for
coming "to see an old nuisance like me." After that one, Marjorie didn't dare look at Pauline again. She did her shopping
and went home in a troubled frame of mind, but she waited
until the children had gone out before opening her heart to her
husband. Seventeen-year-old Brian and sixteen-year-old Susan
were apt, with the ignorance of youth, to remark when their
grandmother was mentioned that Nanna was "a dear old love";
that they wouldn't mind at all if she came to live with them;

and that it was "a drag for Auntie Pauline" never being able to go out.

"Pauline's got a boy friend, George."

"You're joking."

"No, I'm not. He's a doctor she met when she was in that Hightrees place, and he's called round twice in the evenings and stopped ever so late. Mother told me."

"Well, good old Pauline," said George. "She's forty if she's a day."

"She's forty-two," said Marjorie. "You know very well she's seven years younger than I am."

"Doesn't look it though, does she? People always take you for the younger one." George smiled affectionately at his wife and took up the evening paper."

"You're to listen to me, George. Don't read that now. I haven't finished. George, suppose—suppose she was to get married?" The words came out in a breathless, almost hysterical rush. "Suppose she was to marry this doctor?"

"What, old Pauline?"

"Well, why not? I know she's not young and she's nothing to look at, but when you think of the women who do get married. . . . I mean, looks don't seem to have much to do with it. I don't care what these young people say nowadays, *all* women want to get married. So why not Pauline?"

"A man's got to want to marry *them*."

"Yes, but look at it this way. He's a doctor, and Pauline always wanted to be a doctor, only Mother wouldn't have it so she had to settle for nursing instead. And she's got a masculine sort of mind. She can talk way above my head when she wants. They might have a lot in common."

"Good luck to her then, is what I say. She's never so much as been out with a man all the time I've known her, and if she can get herself one now and get married—well, like I said, the best of luck."

"But, George, don't you see? What about Mother? A doctor's bound to have a practice and be overworked and everything.

He wouldn't want Mother. You don't know how awful Mother is. She gets Pauline up five or six times some nights. She rings that bell by her bedside for the least little thing. And when she's up she keeps Pauline on the trot, wanting her glasses or her knitting or her pills. Pauline never complains but sometimes I reckon she'd do anything to get away. I know I shouldn't say it, and yet I wonder if she didn't stage that breakdown when Mother had her first stroke in the hope she'd never have to go back and . . ."

"Aren't you getting steamed up about nothing?" George said placidly. "As far as we know, the bloke's only been there twice and maybe he'll never go there again."

But this was the major worry of Marjorie's life: that the time might come when Mother would have to live with her. She hardly understood how she had managed to escape it so long. From the onset of Mother's illness, she had been the obvious person to care for her. For one thing, she was and always had been Mother's favourite daughter. Pauline was to have been a boy. Even now Marjorie could remember, as a child of seven, Mother saying to her friends, "I'm carrying forward, so it'll be a boy this time." Paul. The name was ready, the blue baby clothes. Mother had never really got over having a second daughter. There had been, Marjorie recalled, some neglect, some degree of cruelty. Scathing words for Pauline when she wanted to take up medicine, cruel words when she had never married. Marjorie had quite a big house, big enough for Mother to have a bed-sitting room of her own; she had no job; her children fended for themselves. How lucky it was for her Pauline hadn't been Paul, for no man would have given up his job, his flat, his whole way of life, to care for an unloved, unloving mother. . . .

While Mother lived, though, it would never be too late for a change. And Marjorie knew she couldn't depend on George and the children for support. Even George would surrender quietly to the invasion of his home by a mother-in-law, for it wouldn't be he Mother would get up in the night or nag about draughts and rheumatism and eyedrops and hot milk. He wouldn't be expected to listen to interminable stories about what things were like in nineteen-ten, or be asked daily in a mournful tone: "D'you think I'll see another winter out, dear?"

She had always, in spite of her seniority, been a little afraid of Pauline. As a child, her sister had been a very withdrawn person, spending long hours shut up in her bedroom. She had had an imaginary friend in those days, one of those not uncommon childhood creations—Marjorie's own Susan had behaved in much the same way—but Pauline's Pablo had persisted almost into her teens, and had always been put forward as the mouthpiece of Pauline's own feelings. "Pablo says he doesn't want to go," when some outing had been proposed on which Pauline herself didn't want to go; "Pablo hates you," when there was a need to express Pauline's own hatred. Pablo from "Pablo the Fisherman," a popular song of the time, Marjorie supposed. He had disappeared at Pauline's puberty, and since then Marjorie couldn't remember her sister once showing her feelings. No, not when Father died or Marjorie's first baby was born dead. And when she had been told that the only alternative to Mother's going into a sixty-pound-a-week nursing home was her abandoning her job and her home, she had said merely, with a blank face, "I suppose I've got no choice, then."

Never once had she suggested Marjorie as an alternative. But the first time Marjorie called at the new Pauline-Mother ménage Pauline, who in the past had always kissed her when they met and parted, made a quiet but marked point of not doing so. And since that day they had never exchanged a kiss. Not when Mother had her second stroke; not when Mother was temporarily in hospital and Marjorie visited Pauline in Hightrees. No complaints about the arduousness of her duties ever escaped Pauline's narrow-set lips, nor would she ever protest to Mother herself, however exigent she might be. Instead, she would sometimes enumerate in a cold, monotonous voice the tasks she had accomplished since the night before.

"Mother got me up at midnight and again at four and five. But she still had a wet bed. I got everything washed out by eight and then I turned out the living room. I went down to

the shops but I forgot Mother's prescription, so I had to go
back for it."

Marjorie would cringe with guilt and shame during this
catalogue and actually shiver when, at the end of it, Pauline
turned upon her large, glazed eyes in which seemed to lurk a
spark of bitter irony. Those eyes said, though the lips never
did, "To her that has shall be given, but from her that has not
shall be taken away even that which she has." Marjorie could
have borne it better, have worried less and agonised less, if
they could have had a real ding-dong battle. But that was impossible with Pauline. Apologise to Pauline for a missed visit
and all she said was "That's O.K. Suit yourself." Tell her to
cheer up and you got "I'm all right. Leave me alone." Offer
sympathy combined with excuses about having your own family to attend to, and you got no answer at all, unless a stare of
profound contempt is an answer. So Marjorie felt she couldn't,
as yet at any rate, tackle Pauline about her doctor friend.

But she was driven to do so a week later. She could see
something had happened to upset Mother the minute she
walked into the room. Mother's mouth was turned down and
she kept looking at Pauline in a truculent, injured kind of way.
And Pauline just sat there, determined not to leave Mother
and Marjorie alone for a moment, although she must have
been able to see Mother was dying to get Marjorie on her own.
But at three the laundryman called, and luckily for Mother,
there seemed to be some problem about a missing pillowcase
which kept Pauline arguing on the step for nearly five minutes.

"That man was here again last night, Marjorie," Mother said,
"and he came into my room and spoke to me. He bullied me,
Marjorie, he said awful things to me."

"What on earth d'you mean, Mother?"

"Oh, dear, I hope she won't come back for a minute. I heard
him talking down here last night. About ten, it was. I'd drunk
my water and Pauline had brought me another glass, but I
couldn't sleep, I was so hot. I rang the bell for Pauline to take
the eiderdown off me. I had to ring and ring before she came
and of course I couldn't help—well, I was feeling a bit weepy

by then, Marjorie." Mother sniffed and gave a sort of gulp. "The next thing I knew that man, that doctor, had marched right into my room and started bullying me."

"But what did he say?"

"He was very rude. He was very impertinent, Marjorie. I wish you'd heard him, I wish you'd been there to stand up for me. Pauline wasn't there, just him shouting at me."

Marjorie was aghast. "What did he *say*?"

"Just because he's a doctor. . . . Doctors don't have the right to say what they like if you're not their patient, do they?"

"Mother, please tell me before Pauline gets back."

"He said I was a very lucky woman and I ought to understand that, and I was selfish and demanding and I'd driven my daughter into a breakdown, and if I didn't stop getting her up in the night she'd have another one and . . . Oh, Marjorie, it was awful. He went on and on in a very deep, bossy sort of voice. I started crying and then I thought he was going to get hold of me and shake me. He just stood there in the doorway against the light, shaking his finger at me and—and *booming* at me and . . ."

"Oh, dear God," said Marjorie. Now she *would* have to speak to Pauline. She sighed wretchedly. Why did this have to happen? Not that she cared very much about what anyone said to Mother—do her good, it was all true anyway—but that someone should point out to Pauline facts which Pauline herself had possibly never realised! Much more of that and . . . She went out into the hall and intercepted Pauline parting from the laundryman.

"Mother's been on about nothing else since first thing this morning," said Pauline.

"Well, I don't wonder. You know I don't like to criticise you, but you really shouldn't let people—I mean, strangers—upset Mother."

Pauline dumped the heavy laundry box on the kitchen table. She looked even more tired than usual. Her skin had a battered appearance as if lack of sleep and peace and recreation had actually dented and bruised it. She shrugged.

"You believe her? You take all that rubbish for gospel?"

"You mean you don't have a friend who's a doctor? He didn't go into Mother's room and boss her about last night? It's all her imagination?"

"That's right," said Pauline laconically, and she filled the kettle. "She imagined it, she's getting senile."

"But Mother never had any imagination. She heard him. She *saw* him."

"She can't see," said Pauline. "Or not much. It was a dream."

For a moment Marjorie was certain that she was lying. But you could never tell with Pauline. And what was more likely, after all? That Pauline, who had everything to gain in esteem and interest by having a man friend should deny his existence, or that Mother, who was eighty and half blind and maybe senile like Pauline said, should magnify a nightmare into reality? Could it be, Marjorie wondered, that it had been Mother's conscience talking? That was very far-fetched, of course, what her son and daughter would call way-out—but if only it were true! The alternative was almost too unpleasant to face. It took George to put it into words.

"Old Pauline's always been a dark horse. I can see what game she's playing. She's keeping him in the background till he's popped the question."

"Oh, George, no! But she did look very funny when I spoke about him. And, George, the awful thing is, if he does marry Pauline he'll never have Mother to live with them when he feels like that about her, never."

Worrying about it brought on such a headache that when the time came for her next duty visit, Marjorie had to phone Mother's house and say she couldn't come over. A man's voice answered.

"Hallo?"

"I'm sorry, I think I've got a wrong number. I wanted to speak to Miss Needham."

"Miss Needham is lying down, having a well-earned rest." The voice was deep, cultured, authoritative. "Is that by any chance Mrs Crossley?"

Marjorie said breathlessly that it was. But she was too taken aback to ask if her mother was all right, and who was he, anyway? She cared very little about the answer to the first question and she knew the answer to the second. Besides, he had interrupted her reply by launching into a flood of hectoring.

"Mrs Crossley, as a doctor I don't think I'm overstepping the bounds of decorum by telling you that I think you personally take a very irresponsible attitude to the situation here. I've hoped for an opportunity to tell you so. There seems to me, from what your sister tells me, no reason at all why you shouldn't share some of the burden of caring for Mrs Needham."

"I don't, I . . ." Marjorie stammered, thunderstruck.

"No, you don't realise, do you? Perhaps you haven't cared to think about it too deeply. Your mother is a very demanding woman, a very selfish woman. I have spoken to her myself, though I know from experience that it is almost useless telling home truths to someone of her age and in her condition."

So it was true, after all. Marjorie felt a spurt of real rage against Pauline. "I should have thought it was for my mother's own doctor," she blustered. "I don't know what an outsider . . ."

"An *outsider?*" She might have levelled at him some outrageous insult. "I am a close friend of your sister, Mrs Crossley, perhaps the only true friend she has. Please don't speak of *outsiders*. Now if you have any feeling for your sister, I'm sure you'll appreciate . . ."

"I don't want to talk about it," Marjorie almost shouted. Her head was splitting now. "It's no business of yours and I don't want to discuss it."

She told George.

"He said he was a close friend, her only true friend. They're cooking this up together, George. He means to marry her, but he'll get Mother out of the way first. He'll foist Mother on to me and then they'll get married and. . . . Oh, George, what am I going to do?"

Not see Mother or Pauline, at any rate. Marjorie extended

her headache over the next two visiting times, and after that she half-invented, half-suffered, a virus infection. Of course, she had to phone and explain, and it was with a trembling hand that she dialled the number in case that awful man should answer. He didn't. Pauline was more abrupt than ever. Marjorie didn't mention her doctor friend, though she fancied, just as she was replacing the receiver, that she heard the murmur of his voice in the background talking to Mother.

It was George and Brian together who at last paid a visit to Mother's house. Marjorie was in bed when they came back, cowering under the sheets and trying to make the mercury in her thermometer go above ninety-eight by burying it in her electric blanket.

They hadn't, they said, seen Pauline's friend, but Nanna had been full of him, now entirely won over to him as a charming man, while Pauline, as she talked, had sat looking very close with an occasional flash of impatience in her eyes.

"He's got some Russian name," said George, though he couldn't remember what it was, and Brian kept talking nonsense about dogs and reactions and other things Marjorie couldn't follow. "He lives in Kensington, got a big practice. One of those big houses on Campden Hill. You know where I mean. Pauline did a private nursing job in one of them years ago. Quite a coincidence."

Marjorie didn't want to hear about coincidences.

"Is he going to marry her?"

"I reckon," said Brian, "going from the way Nanna talks about what he says."

"What *do* you mean?"

"Well, Auntie Pauline went off to get us coffee and while she was outside Nanna said he's always telling her how lovely her daughter is and what a fine mind and how she's wasted and all that."

"Nanna must have changed. She's never had a good word to say for your auntie."

"She *is* changed," said George. "She's all for Pauline going off and leading her own life and her coming here to live with us. Dr Whatsit's told her it would be a good idea, you see. And I must say, Marge, it might be the best thing in the long run. If Nanna sold her house and let us have some of the money and we had an extension built on . . ."

"And I'll be off to university in the autumn," put in Brian.

"I never did think it quite fair," said George, "poor old Pauline having to bear the whole burden of Nanna on her own. It's not as if they ever really got on and . . ."

"Nanna's an old love with people she gets on with," said Brian.

"I won't do it, I won't!" Marjorie screamed. "And no one's going to make me!"

For a little while no one attempted to. Marjorie prolonged her illness, augmenting it with back pains and vague menopausal symptoms, for as long as she could. Mother never used the telephone, and Marjorie could have counted on the fingers of one hand the number of times Pauline had phoned her in the past two years. Now there was no communication between the two houses. Marjorie began to go out again but she avoided going near Mother's, and her own family, George and Brian and Susan, wishing perhaps to prevent a further outburst of hysterics, kept off the subject of her mother. Until one day George said, "I had a call at work from that doctor friend of Pauline's."

"I don't want to know, George," said Marjorie. "It's no business of his. I've told you I won't have Mother here and I won't."

"As a matter of fact," her husband admitted, "he's phoned me a couple of times before, only I didn't tell you, seeing how upset it makes you."

"Of course it upsets me. I'm ill."

"No, you're not," said George with unexpected firmness. "You're as right as rain. A sick woman couldn't eat a meal like the one you've just eaten. It's Pauline who's ill, Marge. She's cracking up. He told me in the nicest possible way; he's a very decent chap. But we have to do something about it."

"Any other man," said Marjorie tearfully, "would be thankful to have a wife who stopped her mother coming to live with them."

"Well, I'm not any other man. I don't mind the upheaval and the extra expense. We'll all do our bit, Brian and Sue too. Don't you see, it's our *turn*. Pauline's had two years of it. The doctor says she'll have another breakdown if we don't, and God knows what might be the outcome."

"You're all against me," Marjorie sobbed, and because he was her husband and she didn't much care what she said in front of him, "Pauline's got pills from her nursing days, morphine and I don't know what. There ought to be—what's it called?—euthanasia. There ought to be a way of putting people like Mother out of their misery."

He looked at her, his eyes narrowing. "There isn't. Maybe dogs are luckier than people. There isn't a geriatric hospital that'll take her either. There's no one but us, Marge, so you'd better turn off the waterworks and make up your mind to it."

She saw how it would be. It would take months for Mother to sell her house and get the money for an extension to theirs, a year perhaps before that extension was built. Even when it was built and Mother was installed, things would be bad enough. But before that . . . ! Her dining room turned into a bedroom, every evening spoiled by the business of getting Mother to bed, nights that would be even worse than when Brian and Susan were babies. And she wasn't thirty any more. The television turned down to a murmur once Mother was in bed, her shopping times curtailed, her little afternoon visits to the cinema over for good. Marjorie wondered if she would have the courage to throw herself downstairs, break a leg, so that they would understand having Mother was out of the question. But she might break her neck. . . .

And all the while this was going on, Pauline would be living in the splendour of Campden Hill, Mrs Something Russian, with a new husband, an educated, important, rich man. Giving parties. Entertaining eminent surgeons and professors and what not. Going abroad. It was unbearable. She might lack the courage to throw herself downstairs, but she thought she could be brave enough to confront Pauline here and now and tell her No. No, I won't. You took it on, you must go through with it. Crack up, break down, go crazy, die. Yes, die before I'll ruin my life for you.

Of course, she wouldn't put it like that. She would be firm and kind. She would even offer to sit with Mother sometimes so that Pauline could go out. Anything, anything, except that permanency which would trap her as Pauline had been trapped.

Things are never as we imagine they will be. No situation ever parallels our prevision of it. Marjorie, when she at last called, expected an irate, resentful Pauline, perhaps even a Pauline harassed by wedding plans. She expected Mother to be bewildered by the proposed changes in her life. And both, she thought, would be bitter against her for her long absence. But Mother was just the same, pleased to see her, anxious to get her alone for those little whispered confidences, even more anxious to know if she was better. Her purblind eyes searched Marjorie's face for signs of debility, held her hand, pressed her to wrap up warm.

Anyone less like a potential bride than Pauline Marjorie couldn't have imagined. She seemed thinner than ever, and her face, bruise-dark, patchily shadowed, lined like raisin skin, reminded her of pictures she had seen of Indian beggars. Marjorie followed her into the kitchen when she went to make tea and gathered up her courage.

"How have you been keeping, Pauline?"

"All right. Just the same." And although she hadn't been asked, Pauline said, "Mother had me up four times in the night. She fell over in the passage and I had to drag her back to bed. The laundry didn't come, so I did the sheets myself. It's a job getting them dry when it's raining like today."

"I was thinking, I could come in two evenings a week and sit with her so that you could go out. There's no reason why I shouldn't take some of the washing and do it in my machine. Come to that, I could take it all. Every week."

Pauline shrugged. "Suit yourself."

"Yes, well, it's all very well saying that," said Marjorie, working herself up to the required pitch, "but if you keep on complaining like this, what am I to say?"

"I don't complain."

"Maybe not. But everyone else does. You know very well who I mean. I can't take all this outside interference and just pretend it's not happening."

"I shouldn't call a husband outside interference."

For a moment Marjorie thought she was referring to George. Realisation of what she actually meant gave her the impetus she needed. "I may as well tell you straight out, Pauline, I'm not having Mother to live with us and that's flat. I'll do anything else in my power, but not that. No one can make me and I shan't."

Pauline made no answer. They ate their tea in almost total silence. Marjorie couldn't remember ever having felt so uncomfortable in the whole of her life. On the doorstep, as she was leaving, she said, "You'd better tell me which evenings you want me, and you can let me know when you want George to come round in the car for the washing."

"It makes no difference to me," said Pauline. "I'm always here."

Of course, she didn't phone. Marjorie knew she wouldn't. And what was the point of going round in the evening when Pauline didn't want to go out, when she was snug at home with her doctor?

"We're not having Mother," she said to George. "That's definite. I've cleared it all up with Pauline. She's quite capable of carrying on if I help out a bit."

"That's not what I was told."

"It's what I'm telling you." Marjorie hated the way he looked at her these days, with a kind of dull, distasteful reproach. "She's done the washing for this week, and next week the laundry'll do the sheets and the heavy stuff. I thought we might go over on Friday and collect their bits and pieces, put them in my machine."

So on Thursday Marjorie phoned. She chose the morning

just in case that man might answer. Doctors are never free to make social calls in the morning. Pauline answered.

"O.K. Tomorrow, if you like."

"It's what *you* like, Pauline," said Marjorie, feeling that her sister might at least have said thank you.

She added that they would be there at seven. But by seven George hadn't yet got home, so Marjorie dialled her mother's number. It didn't matter if *he* answered. Show him she wasn't the indifferent creature he took her for. He did. And he was quite polite. Mr and Mrs Crossley couldn't get there till eight-thirty? Never mind. He would still be there and would be delighted to meet them at last.

"We're going to get a look at him at last," said Marjorie to George as he came in at the door. "Now don't you forget, I expect you to back me up if we have any more nonsense about us having Mother and all that. United we stand, divided we fall."

Mother's house was in darkness and the hall light didn't come on when Marjorie rang the bell. She rang it again, and then George rang it.

"Have you got a key?" said George.

"In my bag. Oh, George, you don't think . . . ? I mean . . . ?

"I don't know, do I? Let's get this door open."

No one in the hall or in any of the downstairs rooms. Marjorie, who had turned on lights, began to climb the stairs with George behind her. Halfway up, she heard a man's voice, speaking soothingly but with authority. It came from Mother's room, the door of which was ajar.

"It was the best thing, Pauline. I gave her two hundred milligrammes crushed in her milk drink. She didn't suffer. She just fell asleep, Pauline."

Marjorie gave a little gasping whimper. She clutched George, clawing at his shoulder. As he pushed past her, she heard the voice come again, the same words repeated in the same lulling hypnotic tone.

"I gave her two hundred milligrammes crushed in her milk drink. She didn't suffer. It was the only thing. I did it for you, Pauline, for us. . . ."

George threw open the bedroom door. Mother lay on her back, her face waxen and slack in death, her now totally sightless eyes wide open. There was no one else in the room but Pauline.

Pauline got up as they entered, and giving them a nod of quiet dignity, she placed her fingers on Mother's eyes, closing the lids. Marjorie stared in frozen, paralysed terror, like one in the presence of the supernatural. And then Pauline turned from the bed, came forward with her right hand outstretched.

In a deep, cultured, and authoritative voice, a voice whose hectoring manner on the telephone was softened now by sympathy for the bereaved, she said, "How do you do? I am Dr Pavlov. It's unfortunate we should meet under such sad circumstances but . . ."

Marjorie began to scream.

ALSO BY RUTH RENDELL

A DEMON IN MY VIEW

In this dark and compelling tale, a lonely paranoid sneaks into the basement to visit the object of his affection and slips his hands around her throat, but one day he goes down there and she is gone, and he comes unhinged.

Crime Fiction/0-375-70491-4

HARM DONE

After two girls have disappeared, the people of Kingsmarkham are understandably alarmed. The situation becomes even more ominous when the father of one of the children is stabbed to death, and Wexford finds that in the case of the inner life of families, justice is never as straightfoward as the letter of the law.

Crime Fiction/0-375-72484-2

A JUDGEMENT IN STONE

In this raw and powerful psychological thriller, it only takes housekeeper Eunice fifteen minutes to kill her employer and his family, but for the police to find out why may be a trickier matter—that the tragedy began with a secret Eunice has guarded her whole life.

Crime Fiction/0-375-70496-5

THE LAKE OF DARKNESS

Martin Urban is a quiet bachelor with a comfortable life. When he unexpectedly comes into a small fortune, he wants to share the wealth. But when he helps strangers in need, his good intentions become fatally entangled with the madness of a small-time assassin.

Crime Fiction/0-375-70497-3

MURDER BEING ONCE DONE

A young girl is found murdered in a gloomy cemetery. The authorities, commanded by Inspector Wexford's nephew, can't find out who the victim was: the dead girl has no possessions, no past, and a name that seems patently false. And so Inspector Wexford defies doctor's orders and the big-city condescension of the London police to take a look for himself.

Crime Fiction/0-375-70488-4

NO MORE DYING THEN

Years as a policeman in the placid village of Kingsmarkham have taught Inspector Wexford that the most unlikely people are capable of the most appalling crimes. But what kind of person would steal—and possibly murder—two children? Wexford's search is complicated when his colleague falls in love with the mother of one of the missing youngsters.

Crime Fiction/0-375-70489-2

ONE ACROSS, TWO DOWN

Two things interest Stanley Manning: crossword puzzles and his mother-in-law's money. One afternoon, he lends death a helping hand, but after the deed is done, he realizes that he may get more than he bargained for: a victim who may outsmart him from the grave.

Crime Fiction/0-375-70494-9

SHAKE HANDS FOREVER

Probably, Angela Hathall had picked up a stranger. Probably, the stranger had killed her. It was that simple. Or was it? Inspector Wexford had his doubts—especially after meeting the loved ones Mrs. Hathall left behind.

Crime Fiction/0-375-70495-7

A SLEEPING LIFE

Her corpse is unremarkable, her handbag devoid of clues. But as Inspector Wexford tracks down the few people who knew Rhoda Comfrey before her death, he discovers that even an obscure soul harbors extraordinary secrets.

Crime Fiction/0-375-70493-0

SOME LIE AND SOME DIE

In spite of the dire predictions, the rock festival seems to be going off smoothly. Then a hideously disfigured body is discovered in a nearby quarry. The victim is a local girl who lied about her friendships with celebrities. But she had a very real connection with the festival's charismatic star, a singer who inspires an unwholesome devotion in his followers.

Crime Fiction/0-375-70490-6